Copyright: © 2017 by Lynn Nodima, all rights reserved

First edition published 2017
Cover Design: © 2017, Linda Pogue
Updated Cover: © 2019, Linda Pogue

This cover is based on a design given to the author by Derek Murphy. Thank you, Derek, for all your help in learning more about cover design.

All characters and events are fiction.

This book is copyrighted by the author. Please respect the author's work in writing this book. If you wish to share it, please recommend it to your friends. And don't forget to review it after you finish reading! Thank you!

Wolf's Reign

Lynn Nodima

Dedication

This book is dedicated to my grandchildren, Charles, Naomi, Arianna, Elizabeth, Melody, and Jesse.

Never let anyone convince you that you can't achieve your dreams!

Please Leave a Review

Reviews are the lifeblood of books. After reading this book, please take the time to leave an honest review.

Reviews are not book reports. They are just a few words to let other readers know how you liked or didn't like the book.

Authors, especially indie authors, depend on reviews to help readers find their books. Reviews help an author on the journey.

Chapter 1

Unable to sleep, Nate Rollins, Alpha of the Texas Ranch Wolf Pack, stared through the dark room at the ceiling. Janelle's head was on his shoulder. She mumbled against his chest. He tightened his arm around his mate and his fingers clutched into a fist. Ophelia's soft whimpers reached him through the open door connected to the nursery. Careful not to wake Janelle, Nate forced his fist to relax, slipped his arm from beneath her, then padded barefooted to the nursery.

"Shhh," he whispered to Ophelia, his fingers stroking her tiny chest. "Don't wake Mommy." With expertise born of much practice, he quickly changed her wet diaper, then picked her up and carried her to the rocking chair he bought Janelle soon after they learned she was expecting.

Giving Ophelia a bottle while he rocked slowly back and forth, Nate stared out the window at the moonlit yard. Somewhere in the woods, an owl hooted. Bats swirled through the air, their silhouettes stark against the bright moon. He sighed and looked at his daughter. Koreth's pride in her matched his own, though lately, it was difficult to feel or hear anything from Koreth. Almost as if there was a padded wall between them.

The wolf is not needed.

Nate stopped rocking and sat forward. "What?" he hissed into the darkness.

The wolf is not needed. I am enough.

Lycos. It had to be Lycos. No one else could enter his thoughts so easily. *Koreth is part of me. As much a part of me as you are.*

The rumble of laughter in Nate's mind set him on edge. *I am more powerful than either of you. I am enough. I don't need you.*

Shoving Lycos out of his mind, Nate stood and walked to the bedroom. "Janelle, wake up." He bumped the edge of the bed with his knee. "Wake up!"

"Wha...what?" Blinking, sleep in her eyes, Janelle sat up. Her blonde hair glimmered in the moonlight streaming through the open window. "Nate? What's wrong?"

"Ophelia needs you." He leaned over his mate and transferred his daughter and her bottle to Janelle. "I have to go."

Janelle settled Ophelia in her arms, then looked up at Nate, concern on her shadowed face. "Go where?"

"Out. I have to go out." He saw in her expression she needed him to stay. She wanted him to answer her questions. Neither of which he could do. At least not now. Without another word, Nate spun on his heel and left. Remembering at the last minute there were dozens of people sleeping in the house, Nate shut the front door with a soft click. He jumped off the porch and ran toward the cave where he and Janelle found the surviving pack members when Nate first learned he was *were*.

Going through the back way by vehicle would take almost an hour but running straight through the trees Nate was there in twenty minutes. He slogged through the creek in his bare feet, ignoring the water soaking his flannel pajama bottoms and ducked into the low cave entrance. The cave was left provisioned just in case it was ever again needed as a hideaway. Sooner or later, someone would find him here, but for a short time, he would be alone with his thoughts. He turned on one of the battery-powered lamps left behind and sat on the cot.

Soon after he left his job as a detective in the San Antonio PD and took on Alpha responsibilities for the ranch, he learned he could separate his human and wolf halves into two beings. Closing his eyes, he reached inside, searching for Koreth. Wolfish whines led him to the virtual dungeon Lycos built in his mind. Reaching a hand toward Koreth, he gritted his teeth and felt his jaw clench. Slowly, he forced his hand through the thick imprisoning air surrounding Koreth. Closing a mental hand on the nape of Koreth's neck, he pulled steadily until Koreth passed through the viscous, invisible prison walls.

As soon as Koreth was free of Lycos' prison, Nate commanded they be two. Koreth shimmered into existence in front of him. The wolf shuddered and crowded against Nate's legs. *Lycos trapped me!*

Why would he do that?

Anger blazed in the wolf's eyes. *He is trying to take over. We must not allow him. Janelle, Nadrai, and Ophelia will be helpless against him.*

Nate ruffled the fur behind Koreth's ears. "We'll find a way to stop him." Avoiding thoughts of his doubts and fears, Nate stretched out on the cot. Koreth jumped up and snuggled beside him, nose resting on his paws. His hand resting on Koreth's shoulder, Nate closed his eyes.

In the back of his mind, his massive wolfman form surged against the constraints Nate placed on him. Nate reinforced his hold on Lycos. "We have to find a way."

Even so, hours passed before he had enough control to dare sleep.

*****

Snarl stopped at the edge of the creek and sniffed. *Alpha!* With a slight nod, he sloshed through the creek, ignoring the water filling his boots. At the cave mouth, he hesitated, then shrugged and pushed his way in. If Nate didn't want him in the cave, he would send him home. But something was wrong. Snarl could feel it in his bones. His wolf cowered, as if afraid. Something he had never done in all Snarl's long life.

Inside, a dim battery lamp barely cast enough light to fill the interior. Snarl walked to the shelf and picked up another lamp with fresh batteries, then pressed the switch to flood the cave with more light. He turned to find Nate sleeping on the cot, Koreth stretched out beside him. Koreth raised his head. After a moment, he tilted his head to the left and whined.

Snarl walked to the wolf. "It's okay, Koreth. Let's see what's wrong with the Alpha." Surprised his voice didn't wake Nate, Snarl hesitated. It wasn't a good idea to be too close to a battle-hardened, former Marine commissioned officer when they waken suddenly. Sighing, ready to jump back, Snarl pressed a hand to the Alpha's shoulder. "Nate?" Snarl shook his shoulder. "Nate?"

Nate moaned, then opened one eye. "Snarl? What's up?"

Snarl frowned. The Nate he knew would come up fighting if awakened from a deep sleep. "That's what I want to know. What're you doing out here? You and Janelle have a fight?"

Nate shook his head, then gently nudged Koreth off the cot so he had room to sit up. Koreth jumped to the cave floor and sat, head tilted, tongue hanging out, and looked at Nate. "I'm okay, Koreth." One hand reached out to scratch behind Koreth's ear. "Something happen, Snarl?"

"Yeah. For some reason, the Alpha has gone missing. Know where he is?"

"Very funny. I'm right here."

"Uh huh. But something is bothering you. What's up?"

Snarl endured the steady stare Nate sent him. Nate's bloodshot eyes were haunted. Sitting on a camp stool, Snarl leaned forward. "I've pledged loyalty to you, Alpha. Let me help."

Nate sighed and nodded. Reaching back, he swiped his hand as if reaching for his hip pocket. Surprise filled his eyes and he looked down. "I'm still in my pajamas."

"Uh huh." Snarl scratched the back of his head. "Not often you wander around without all your clothes. Want to tell me about it?"

"I couldn't sleep."

When Nate stopped, Snarl raised an eyebrow at the younger man. "And?"

Nate stood and started pacing barefoot around the cave, walking around the stone-enclosed fire circle. Snarl watched, quiet, waiting for Nate to decide to talk. Two times, then three, the Alpha walked around the circle. When his feet came to an abrupt halt, Snarl studied his face. Stress openly creased his forehead beneath the uncombed dark brown hair.

"Snarl, when we opened the safe and found the second medallion, there was a paper with it." Nate bit his lip then shook his head. "It said, 'Beware the medallion, lest it binds. Valor and strength prevail.' It seemed silly, so I forgot it. When Jackson's medallions melded to mine, and the Progenitors granted me life, I forgot the note...until..."

"Until?"

Nate bowed his head, then lifted it only enough for Snarl to see the angst in his eyes. "Lycos is trying to take over. Control both me and Koreth." He pressed his hands on the knees of his pajamas. "I think that's what the note was about, but I don't wear one medallion, Snarl. I wear four." He raised his head more, his anguished gaze settling on Snarl's eyes. "I think I'm losing this fight."

Snarl motioned toward the bunk Nate slept on. "Sit down, Alpha. We need to talk."

Chapter 2

Blinking against the sweat stinging her eyes, Janelle Rollins twisted to the side. A blade narrowly missed her ribs. She thrust her dagger at the other woman. Her opponent slid to the left, and Janelle's dagger pierced the empty air. Breath coming in short gasps, Janelle jumped back, just avoiding the blade sweeping toward her. Her foot slipped on the dew-wet grass, and her back slapped the ground with enough force to stun her. Squinting into the hot Texas morning sun, she moaned as Zoe stood over her, flipped the knife in her hand, and dropped it into the scabbard on her belt.

Zoe leaned over Janelle and offered her a hand. "Much better, Janelle. You were doing great until you slipped."

Janelle clasped Zoe's wrist and let the younger woman pull her to her feet. Wiping the sweat from her face with the back of her left hand, she grimaced. "If you were the enemy, I'd be dead."

Zoe's cheerful smile was only one of the morning's annoyances. "True, but this is the first time you've lasted more than a few minutes. You're getting better, even if you don't think so." A whistle sounded from the house, and Zoe's pale blonde hair whipped as she turned to look at Daryll, her mate.

Still struggling to catch her breath, Janelle waved at the Enforcer walking toward the two women. She hid a grin. Daryll preferred to work as a carpenter, but his skills as an Enforcer for the pack were too valuable to put aside. At least until after the coronation. Daryll reached them and spun Zoe around before setting her on her feet and giving her a loud, smacking kiss.

He glanced at Janelle, then looked back down at his petite mate. "How's she doing with training?"

"She's a natural. If she continues with the training exercises, she'll be ready."

Janelle sniffed and motioned toward herself. "She's right here!" When Zoe bit her lip, hiding her smile, Janelle sighed. "And she's ready for coffee. It's too early to be this hot and being coffee-less makes it worse."

Zoe leaned against Daryll and grinned at her. "Sorry, Janelle. We're done for this session. Think we might snag a cup of that coffee, too?"

"No problem. I'm sure somebody made coffee this morning." She cut her eyes at Zoe. "If it's not all gone by now."

Daryll snickered. "Someone's grumpy."

Rolling her eyes, Janelle turned and walked across the backyard to the kitchen. "Ophelia fussed all night, so I didn't get much sleep."

Daryll stepped past Janelle and held the kitchen door open for the two women. "Is she teething?"

"No. At least I don't think so. She didn't seem to be hurting anywhere, she just seemed frightened." Janelle motioned for Daryll and Zoe to sit at the bar while she pulled open the cabinet and retrieved three coffee mugs.

Daryll accepted the coffee Janelle handed to him and gave it to Zoe. "Maybe she feels the stress in the pack?"

Zoe blew on the coffee, then took a careful sip. Eyebrow raised, she glanced at Janelle. "Baby wolves can do that?"

"I don't know." Janelle handed Daryll's mug to him, then sat across the bar from them and lifted one shoulder. "I wasn't around the pups much until they were school-aged." Janelle stared down into her mug, watching the reflection from the overhead lights. "None of the pack mothers survived the massacre, so I don't have anyone to ask." Her frown deepened. "Nadrai is uncertain what to do, too."

Daryll took a sip of coffee. "Maybe Renate knows someone who can provide information for you."

"Maybe." Janelle considered calling her sister-in-law, then shrugged and set her mug on the bar. With the tip of her right forefinger, she drew invisible circles on the marble bar top beside her mug, worry bringing her shoulders forward and her head down.

Zoe put her hand on top of Janelle's. Surprised at the contact, Janelle looked up. "What?"

"Something's wrong, Janelle. What is it?"

Looking out the sliding glass door, Janelle sighed. "That obvious, huh?"

"Yeah. What's up?"

"I don't know." At the look Zoe sent her, Janelle shrugged. "I really don't. Nate..., well, he's not himself the last week or so."

Daryll leaned forward. "Have you talked with him?"

"I tried. The closer it gets to having the other Alphas show up, the tenser he gets." She shook her head and laughed. Even in her own ears, the laugh sounded brittle. "Nadrai doesn't understand what's happening to him, either. Koreth barely communicates with her, and Nate won't talk to me."

Zoe let Janelle pull her hand away and gave a sad smile. "He's got a lot on his mind, Janelle. If this coronation isn't handled just right, he could lose everything, including you and Ophelia."

The bear speaks the truth. Sighing, Janelle accepted Nadrai's assessment. She decided she dwelt on it long enough. Lacing her fingers behind her head, she stretched, trying to loosen tight muscles in her back and shoulders. "When do the arrivals start showing up?"

"Tomorrow." Zoe motioned toward Daryll. "We have the desk first since Nate didn't want humans at the desk when the other shifters arrive."

"Both of you? Are we expecting trouble, then?" When the two werebears didn't answer, Janelle set her coffee cup down and leaned toward them. "What is it you aren't telling me?"

Zoe opened her mouth, and Daryll placed his hand on his mate's hand. She clamped her mouth shut, lips pulled between her teeth. Janelle turned her annoyed gaze on Daryll. "What is it you're hiding from me, Daryll?"

He sighed. "We don't know what to expect, Janelle. It's been decades since some of these alphas have been to a meeting. Centuries for others. I think some won't be happy they were 'ordered' to show up. We just don't know and want to be ready for whatever happens."

Chapter 3

Ajoni stepped from the courtesy car that picked him up at the San Antonio International Airport over two hours ago and frowned at the quaint Texas Bay Inn before him. With a jaundiced eye, he glanced at his beta, Kabarl and his brother, Seringi. "Here? We are to stay here?"

"Yes, Highness. This is the hotel reserved for those meeting with the usurper." Kabarl's dark eyes gleamed in the Texas sun. Behind Kabarl, Seringi quietly surveyed the property.

Annoyed, Ajoni bared his teeth at Seringi. No doubt his brother was trying to find a way to take the throne. With feline grace, Ajoni slinked into the hotel lobby, Kabarl at his side, Seringi and two armed bodyguards behind them. Decorated with deep, rich chocolate colors with subtle hints of terracotta and dark turquoise, the hotel lobby sported a Texas theme. Deer antler sconces provided muted lighting from the walls, while a large antler chandelier adorned with lights provided the main lighting for the large room. On the right, a large painting showed cowboys riding herd. Along the back, a waist-high wall enclosed a dining area with seating for fifty or more.

An elevator set into the wall at the end of the marble check-in desk provided easy access to the upper floors, while a door next to the elevator displayed a sign that read Stairs. Ajoni cast a disdainful glance around the room. While clean and attractive, it certainly did not meet the standards for entertaining international royalty.

Kabarl marched to the unmanned desk and slammed his palm on the bell. "We are here!"

A frazzled-looking young woman rushed from the back, followed by a tall, stout, muscular man who leaned against the wall and watched. Ajoni's nose twitched. Bear! Eyes narrowed, he studied the bear's calm regard, then turned to look again at the desk clerk. Wisps of her blonde hair escaped a messy bun and floated around her face. Compared to the ebony tone of Kabarl's arm, the woman's face was pale.

With a slight smirk, head tilted to the side, Ajoni directed soft words to Seringi. "Bring her to my room."

"Not happening!"

Eyebrow raised, Ajoni looked again at the bear. He stood in a fighting stance, his gaze directed at Ajoni. The woman's exasperated sigh brought Ajoni's gaze back to her. She glared at the bear. "I can ask Nate to replace you."

The werebear looked at her, then shrugged. "You can ask. I'm not leaving, Zoe."

"I can take care of myself, Daryll."

"You can, but you won't do it alone." He took a step forward and placed both hands on the service desk. Ignoring her, he glared into Ajoni's eyes. "The King forbids mate challenges during the gathering."

Ajoni brushed nonexistent lint from his jacket. "The usurper has no authority over me."

"And yet you came to his call."

At the bear's caustic tone, Kabarl stepped between the desk and Ajoni. "You will speak to King Ajoni with respect and show deference."

"Yeah? When pigs fly."

"Daryll!"

Kabarl leaped over the desk. His left hand darted forward, caught Daryll by the throat, and lifted him off the floor. The bear laughed in Kabarl's face, his large hand wrapped around the lion's wrist. Kabarl raised his right hand for a killing blow, then froze. Ajoni frowned.

The woman leaned into Kabarl's back. "Let him go or die."

Ajoni snickered. Without moving her blade from Kabarl's back, the blonde woman glanced at Ajoni. A woman unafraid to attack. Unafraid to kill. Intriguing. "Enough. Kabarl, release him. And you, woman, put away the dagger."

Zoe waited until Daryll's feet were both on the ground and Kabarl dropped his hands away from him before she stepped back, dagger still in her hand. "Back on the customer side of the desk."

Kabarl snarled at her, then glanced at Ajoni for orders. Ajoni gave him a slight head-tilted nod. Kabarl stepped back against the desk, used his hands to lift himself to a sitting position, twisted around, dropped to the floor on the other side, then spun to face the woman. Ajoni chuckled. Though he couldn't see the glare Kabarl sent the woman, he saw it enough over the years to know it was there.

Ajoni took a step closer to the desk, his gaze on the werebear. He sniffed again, then grinned. "Ah, you are both bears."

Zoe threw a warning look at Daryll, then turned back to face the Serengeti Pride King. She put three small envelopes holding room key cards on the desk. "Your rooms are one-fifteen, one-sixteen, and one-seventeen. Rooms one-fifteen and one-sixteen have a connecting door. Divide them up among your party as you wish. Your rooms are down the hall to the right."

For a tense moment, no one moved, then Kabarl slid the cards off the desk into his hand. "You will have our bags brought to our rooms."

She crossed her arms and huffed at him, the right side of her lip lifting. "No, I won't. You can take them to your rooms yourself or do without them."

This time, Ajoni laughed out loud. "So, this is your famous American hospitality."

The woman's lips pressed into a tight line. "The staff is currently otherwise engaged. And for your information, American hospitality does not include providing women for your use."

Ajoni raised an eyebrow at her tone. When the hulking bear beside her opened his mouth, Ajoni waved a dismissive hand at him. "Seringi, retrieve our baggage."

Face devoid of emotion, Seringi bowed to his king, then snagged the bellman's cart parked beside the door and went out to get their bags. Turning his attention back to the woman, Ajoni smiled. "If kings apologized, I do believe I would owe you one, Miss..." He peered at the name tag on her right shoulder. "Miss Zoe."

"Mrs. And kings are quite capable of apologizing." She gave him the same look his mother gave him when he was very small and not yet king. "Especially when they behave like disrespectful brats."

"I concede. My apologies, Lady. I did not realize a

woman of worth would work a hotel desk."

"In this country, women and men are due respect until they prove they are unworthy."

Ajoni ignored the grin on the bear man's face. With a slight nod, he turned and motioned for Kabarl to lead him to their rooms. When Kabarl started to speak, Ajoni gave a slight shake of his head. There would be time to teach insolent women their roles after the usurper was dealt with. After Ajoni was crowned *Were* King.

Chapter 4

Getting back into the house without being seen in his muddy pajama bottoms wasn't easy. He had to wait until the kids were in school, the teens were on their morning run, and Janelle finished her training. Still, there was no need for anyone to see him half-dressed and filthy from walking through the creek and then down a dusty trail. After a quick shower, Nate dressed and slipped into the office.

He frowned at the laptop screen. After less than three hours sleep last night and his talk with Snarl, he felt unready to deal with the first three cat Alphas Lycos summoned—Ajoni, King of the Serengeti Pride, Izzat, the Patriarch of the Borneo Leap of Clouded Leopards, and Victoria, Queen of the Tennessee Highland Rim Cougar Pride. They checked into the hotel earlier this morning, long before Nate returned from his trip to the cave.

He studied their photos. When he met them, he intended to call them by name. Only nine guests and already problems surfaced. Lycos surged in his mind, trying to take over to deal with the problems. Nate gripped the edge of the table, shaking with the effort to prevent Lycos' manifestation. When he felt Lycos back off, he pinched the bridge of his nose and sighed. Controlling the Lycos part of him was getting harder. At least Koreth was no longer trapped, his familiar presence comforting in Nate's mind. A tap on the office door brought Nate's head up.

Jonathan Dyers, pack Beta, stood in the door, his forehead creased with concern. "See you a minute, Nate?"

"Come on in, Jonathan. Want some coffee?"

"Sure." The big man walked to the counter running along the wall to his right, snagged a cup and glanced at Nate's coffee free desk. "You need some?"

"Yeah. I do." He gave Jonathan a sheepish grin. "I've been so busy, I forgot it was perking."

Jonathan's steady hands poured two cups, then carried them to Nate's desk. Handing one to Nate, he settled into one of the chairs facing the desk and blew on his coffee before taking a cautious sip. "You get Daryll's report?"

"Hmm. I did." Nate sipped his coffee, then set his cup beside the laptop. "Sounds like they're quite a bunch."

"Cecelia called a few minutes ago. She can't find Zoe or Daryll, and the Serengeti Beta is causing problems."

Nate sighed, exasperated. "What kind of problems?"

"Entitlement kinds of problems. That group doesn't seem to understand the rules. Two of the human staff have threatened to quit over inappropriate advances they've received. Three more for unreasonable demands."

With muttered curses, Nate closed the laptop and stood up. "Call and have the conference room prepared, then let's go straighten it out."

"You may need the Enforcers."

"Daryll is already there."

"Yes, but no one can find him. Or Zoe."

Nate bowed his head, thinking, then looked up at Jonathan. "Who was that Council Guard Captain? Riker?" He snapped his fingers. "No, Captain Fischer.

Did you contact him to bring the guard to the meetings?"

"I called him yesterday. They were supposed to be here this afternoon, but they're running early." Jonathan looked at his watch. "Actually, they'll be here in an hour or less."

Thirty minutes later, Nate stood at the head of the conference room, waiting for the last stragglers to come in. Six round cloth covered tables filled the room. Only two were occupied. Overhead, six stag horn chandeliers glowed with dozens of small bulbs. Hushed conversation rippled through the small crowd. Ajoni was late, as was all his staff. Just as Nate tapped the microphone to get everyone's attention, the back doors burst open. Behind Ajoni, Kabarl carried Daryll over his shoulder, while Seringi held Zoe's wrists behind her. Though both the bears were bruised and battered, Zoe's captor held her gently. Nate frowned. Blood dripped from Daryll's forehead to the carpet.

In the sudden silence, Nate closed his eyes until he was sure he had control of Lycos, then stood to his full height, shoulders back, eyes narrowed, watching the Serengeti lions stomp through the room. They stopped less than five paces from Nate. The Alpha's gaze swept over Daryll. Once he was sure the unconscious man was breathing, he looked at Zoe. "Are you okay?"

Zoe nodded without speaking, then glared at the man holding her. Thankful he had memorized all their names. Nate sighed, releasing hope of getting through the meeting without a confrontation. "Put him down, Kabarl. Seringi, let her go. We're late getting this meeting started."

Ajoni waved his fingers. Daryll's body crashed to the floor. Seringi released Zoe, and she rushed to Daryll. A low moan came from Daryll as she gently rolled him over, checking his wounds. His eyes fluttered open. The pride king laughed. "There is no need for a meeting. I challenge!"

Startled gasps filled the room, then it grew quiet again. The air conditioner hummed, working to cool the slight crowd. Ignoring the roar at the back of his mind, Nate nodded. "I accept the challenge, Ajoni, but not here. As the challenged, I choose the ranch as our place of combat." He turned to Jonathan. "Have an SUV brought for each group. We'll move this to the ranch and continue there."

With a nod, Jonathan pulled his cell phone from his pocket and started dialing. He walked out of the room to make the arrangements. The door clicked shut behind him.

Nate's narrowed gaze speared Ajoni. He fought the anger filling his chest, striving to stay in human form, to control Lycos. "We leave in fifteen minutes."

Ajoni sneered. "Be ready to bow to me, if you want to live, Usurper." Spinning on his heel, Ajoni marched out of the room.

Lycos surged, trying to take control. Nate clenched his fists and fought him back, then swept his gaze over the clouded leopards and the cougars. Quiet, they waited to see what he would do. "We'll transport you all to the ranch to witness." He glanced around the room, his gaze touching each person. "I'd hoped we could do without the challenge, but since we can't, if any of you intend to challenge, let Jonathan know. Let's get this done so we can plan for the future."

Ignoring the eyes of the leopards and cougars, Nate squatted beside Zoe and Daryll. "How bad are you hurt?"

Arm pressed tight against his abdomen, Daryll winced and let Zoe help him sit up. "I'll be okay in an hour or so."

"What caused it?"

Daryll's eyes blazed with anger. "They tried to take Zoe to Ajoni. He said she would make an 'excellent concubine.'"

Nate frowned and ran the splayed fingers of his right hand through his hair. He glanced at the young blonde woman. "Are you hurt?"

"Not really, no. Your call to convene came before they had much time with me." Zoe bit her lip. "Nate, if you lose, we'll all be subjects to Ajoni."

Aware of the watching cats, Nate displayed a practiced nonchalance. "Nothing to worry about, Zoe. I won't lose."

"I know. It's just..."

"Worrying?"

Zoe hesitated for a moment, then laughed. "No. I believe in you, Nate. You are the *Were* King we need."

Nate grinned and shrugged. "So, they tell me." When Jonathan stepped back into the room, Nate stood and motioned for him to come over. "Is the Council Guard here, yet?"

"ETA ten minutes."

Nate nodded. "Call Fischer. Have them go straight to the ranch. I want them on hand in case there's trouble during the challenge." Jonathan pulled his phone back out of his pocket. "Oh, and Jonathan? Give the human staff the month off, with double pay, starting this evening. We'll have Fischer and his men take over staff duties at the inn."

Jonathan grinned. "They'll love that."

Chapter 5

North of Broken Bow, Oklahoma, deep in forested hills, the Triumvirate, commanders of the Black Forest Huntsmen reviewed the departure logs for an attack against the Texas Ranch Wolf Pack. Huntsman Colonel Lee Hill stood at attention before the u-shaped table, waiting for orders, sweat running down his back. The Supreme Commander leaned forward, brows low on his forehead. "And none returned, Colonel Hill?"

"Sir, no, Sir! Their locators stopped transmitting over a period of two hours, Sir." None of the terror zinging down the colonel's spine showed in his voice. For the first time, he regretted his swift advance through the ranks at the age of twenty-four. Being the youngest to ever make colonel no longer seemed so grand.

"The wolves killed eight Huntsmen squads?" The Supreme Commander shook his head. "Not possible. They aren't that powerful."

The Subcommander on his right twitched in his chair. "This is not the first group to fail?"

"Sir, no, Sir! A recovery team never returned, and the team that went to Arkansas failed, too, Sir."

"Three attacks. Two states." Startled when the third commander's eyes glowed a sickly whitish yellow color, the colonel almost missed the words when he continued. "And all failed? Training methods are lax, it seems."

Glowing yellow eyes? Swallowing, the Huntsman colonel stared ahead, waiting for questions or orders. Strict training kept his face blank. Events spiraled out of control after the last attack. Friends were among those missing. *Paige is missing. Presumed dead.*

The Triumvirate bent their heads together, their conversation too soft for the major to hear. Several moments passed, then they looked at the Huntsman again. The Supreme Commander stood, his chair rollers rumbling on the floor. "Take a trip, Colonel. See what you can learn. Do not attack. This is reconnaissance only. Find out what is going on in Hallettsville, then return and report. Go alone."

The colonel saluted. "Sir, yes, Sir!"

Without returning his salute, the three Triumvirate Commanders stalked out of the conference room. The colonel stood still until the door clicked shut behind them. Waiting a moment more to make sure they wouldn't return, he finally released a shuddering breath and dropped the salute.

Bowing his head, thoughts of his friends filtered through the shield he erected when they didn't return. Living again his recurring nightmare, seeing the light in Paige Marston's green eyes fade, dulled by death, a werewolf at her throat, wrenched through him. Paige thought of him as a friend, but to him she was everything.

He took another shaky breath, nodded, then whispered. "If you're alive, Paige, I'll find you. If not, I'll avenge you!" Leaving his fierce whisper in the air of the still room, he spun on his heel and marched toward his quarters to grab his go bag.

Chapter 6

Seringi stepped down from the front passenger seat of the SUV transporting the Serengeti lions. A quick visual sweep gave him the basic layout of the ranch compound. *No pack children?* They must be hidden away. *Were* in Council Guard uniforms stood around an empty field. No doubt the location of the challenge fight. Uniformed Enforcers stood guard around the main house.

Opening the rear door, Seringi bowed. Ajoni, his brother and King, jumped from the SUV, looked around, and sniffed. "Quaint."

"Ajoni, you are a guest here."

"I am King here, Seringi. This will make a good summer retreat."

Seringi didn't answer. *He won't listen, anyway. Why did father name him heir to the Pride?* Ajoni's mother always did sway Father too much. Careful to keep his feelings off his face, Seringi glanced at his brother. If Ajoni won, Seringi planned to challenge him. Ajoni's hubris and his methods worked only because the Pride was in such a remote place. If Ajoni became *Were* King, humans everywhere would learn of *were*. *I can't let that happen!*

The clouded leopards and cougars assembled in two small groups. Seringi glanced at each, paying close attention to the leopard Alpha and the cougar Queen. They returned his gaze without challenge, but they didn't bend their necks in submission, either. Seringi sighed. *No trouble from them, then. They just want to see what happens next.*

A loud whistle brought him around. Nate stood at the gate to the field. "The challenge ground is beyond this gate. Only those in the challenge may enter. All others must watch from the fence." He turned to face Ajoni. "You may concede if you choose."

Seringi's lips twitched, and he almost laughed. Ajoni's shouted denial was no surprise. The man didn't have any sense when it came to his personal pride. After sweeping a pensive gaze over Nate, Seringi's apprehension grew. *This man radiates power. Why can't Ajoni sense it?*

Nate bowed and folded his arm across his abdomen, gesturing for Ajoni to precede him into the field. Head high, Ajoni strutted past the wolf Alpha two steps inside the field, then whirled. One of the wolves at the fence gasped when the Serengeti King attacked Nate from behind.

Quick as Ajoni was, the wolf Alpha was quicker. Slipping to the side, he hooked his left foot behind Ajoni's ankle. Ajoni shouted in anger as he sprawled. Rolling to his feet, Ajoni shimmered into lion form, his roar filling the air, and charged.

Nate stood waiting for the lion to reach him. Shifting only his hand to Lycos, he spun aside, his clawed hand catching the lion's mane. A quick twist of his wrist flipped the lion in the air. Before Ajoni landed, Nate threw his head back and shifted to Lycos. His deafening roar made Ajoni sound like a weak kitten.

Ajoni leaped at him. Lycos caught him in his arms. Pulling the lion closer, Lycos wrapped the tight bands of his muscled arms around Ajoni's chest, ignoring the hind claws ripping into his thighs. Ajoni twisted, tried to catch Lycos' neck in his huge mouth, but couldn't get past the shoulder that slammed into his maw.

Lycos' arms squeezed tighter and tighter until Ajoni no longer had the breath to roar. Angry mewling sounds came from the lion, then low moans. Seringi believed Lycos would squeeze until he broke Ajoni's ribs and spine, but when Ajoni quit fighting and started squirming to get away, Lycos threw him twenty feet into the field.

Wounds bleeding, Lycos waited for Ajoni to renew his attack. Ajoni staggered to his feet and shook his head. The Lycos fixed glowing eyes on the lion. "Submit or die."

Seringi caught his breath. Ajoni took a weaving step forward, snarled, then pounced at the Lycos. Lycos stood steady, not moving until the last second. His massive claws snagged Ajoni by the throat. He turned and dove to the ground, taking the lion with him. They rolled together, both using claws to rip flesh from the other. When they stopped, Lycos straddled Ajoni's chest.

"Submit." The word was more roar than language.

Ajoni swiped his claws across Lycos' chest. Lycos caught Ajoni's head in his massive hands, twisted, then jerked. With a loud snap, Ajoni's neck broke. The lion sagged, the life fading from his eyes. Lycos stood. Glaring down at the dying lion, he shook his head.

Lycos looked at Seringi. "I am *Were* King. Submit."

Seringi met the Lycos' hard gaze for a moment. Lycos raised his clawed hand, ready to attack. Seringi tilted his head to the right, baring his neck in submission, and dropped to one knee. "I submit. My pride submits. Hail the King!"

Lycos shimmered into Nate. The shimmer started again. Lycos formed, then with a howl the wolfman's head snapped back. The glow returned. When it dissipated, Nate appeared, the wounds beneath his blood healing during the shift. He took a deep shuddering breath, released it, then looked at the cougar Queen and the leopard Alpha. "I am King. Challenge now or submit."

Clothing rustled behind Seringi, then soft thuds sounded as lions, leopards, and cougars knelt in submission. A dozen voices shouted, "Hail the King!"

Chapter 7

Nate gazed around the large office. Janelle sat next to him at the head of the conference table. Below the table, her hands twisted in her lap. Jonathan stood at the door. The strength of Snarl's presence at the wall behind him was steady, calming. Maybe he could get through this meeting without Lycos. *I hope so, anyway!* He felt Koreth's agreement. Lycos pushed against Nate's mind. Nate blocked him, rolling his shoulders with the effort.

Scattered around the table, the leopard Alpha, the cougar Queen, and Seringi muttered to each other with occasional glances at Nate. Concern displayed on the features of the Serengeti king, assuming Seringi was now king of the Serengeti pride, the Tennessee pride Queen, and the Borneo leap Alpha. Behind each group leader, their seconds and guards stood at attention. After a glance at his mate, Nate's gaze moved to touch each Alpha.

Nate knocked twice on the table. The group stopped their soft murmurs and looked at him. "I intended to have this meeting at the inn, but since you're all here, we might as well get it done. Thank you for coming to Texas. I know it was quite a trip for some of you. I'll reimburse your travel expenses."

He leaned forward, his elbows on the table. "We have some information you need. First, how many of you have had an increasing problem with Hunters?"

The atmosphere changed, as everyone sharpened their gazes. Seringi leaned forward, his left forearm pressed to the table, his ebony fingers drumming. "Why? What do you gain from the answer to this question?"

Nate ignored the question. "Do you know the Black Forest Huntsmen were founded and are controlled by vampires?"

The alphas didn't try to hide their surprise. All the guests started talking at once. Seringi slammed his palm on the conference table. Instantly, there was silence in the room. Nate raised an eyebrow. *So, Snarl was right. Most of the others will follow the lions.*

In the startled silence, Seringi leaned forward. "You have proof?"

"I don't have a vampire to show you, no. But I do have witnesses. Zoe, the female bear your group attacked, is one of the witnesses."

"Witness?"

"She's a changeling. Before that, she was a Huntsmen. While she was with the Huntsmen, the vampires attacked her."

Seringi leaned back, crossed his arms over his chest, and frowned. "You accept Huntsmen as changelings?"

"Occasionally. If it serves our need." Nate gave the werelion a piercing look. "By the way, your delegation owes Zoe and her mate, Daryll, an apology."

"Ajoni ordered her capture. He's dead."

Nate's left thumb drummed on the table. "True, but he wasn't the one beating Daryll or holding Zoe."

Lips pursed, Seringi studied Nate's face. Nate met him stare for stare. Seringi lowered his gaze and nodded. "They will receive apologies."

He leaned toward Nate, looked up again, and motioned toward the other leaders. "Hunters haven't bothered us for the past hundred years, but there have been rumors of them getting braver and more numerous. Tell us more about these vampires."

Chapter 8

Janelle rolled over. Her hand swept out to touch Nate, but he was gone. Again. The sheets were cold. Opening her eyes, she peered through the shadows into the nursery and found him standing over Ophelia's crib. His hand gentle on the infant's head, he stroked her hair while staring out the open window. The muscles on his bare back and shoulders were rigid and tight above his pajama bottoms.

"Are you okay?"

He hesitated, then nodded without looking around.

"Want to talk about it?"

The anguish in his soft sigh wrapped around her heart and brought tears to her eyes. Slipping out of bed, she padded across the soft carpet and wrapped her arms around him from behind. "Nate, you didn't have a choice. You tried to get him to submit. He wouldn't. He'd have killed you."

"I know."

At the pain in his voice. She pressed her forehead to his back. "Don't do this to yourself."

Nate bent to press a light kiss to Ophelia's forehead, then turned and wrapped his arms around Janelle. "If I hadn't called them to come here, he'd still be alive."

"Yes. That's true." Janelle looked up into the misery swimming in his eyes. She bit her lip, then touched his face. "If you hadn't called them to come here, he would still be alive. But, if you don't gather them all beneath one crown, we all die when V-Triumph gains the power to rule the world." She raised on her toes and kissed him, a gentle, consoling kiss, without passion.

He pulled away, his entire body shaking. When he was in control, he looked at Janelle. "Who am I to think I should be the king, Janelle?"

She smiled into his eyes. "You are Nate Rollins, son of Grant and Linette Rollins. You bear the blood of royalty in you."

"I am nothing. I lost again, Janelle. I lost my parents. Dusty abandoned me. My squad died in a helicopter crash that should've killed me, too." He took a deep ragged breath. "I killed my own uncle, and now, I've killed the first to challenge my right as king." He bowed his head and closed his eyes. "I'm nothing, but a killer."

"Oh, Nate." Janelle took his hands and pulled him to the bed. With a gentle shove, she maneuvered him to sit on the edge. Dropping to her knees, she caught his hands in hers. "Look at me."

The pain on his face struck her. She took a deep breath. "You are so much and so important! You're the first in generations to have the full powers of a royal alpha. The first to have the ability to protect us all, shifters and human, from the vampires."

His shrug made her more determined to get through to him. "Nate, your father died protecting you. Your mother married Dusty to give you a legal guardian when she died. Dusty left you in that ice cream shop to keep Jackson from catching you. I know losing your men hurt, but I'm so thankful you survived that crash."

He tried to turn away, and she caught his arm. If he really wanted to go, she couldn't stop him, but Nate wouldn't hurt her. Ever. Not on purpose, and not physically. The ache threatening to send tears down her face was not physical, though. "Nate."

She waited until he looked at her. "Jackson was evil. A man who hurt and killed for pleasure, as was his son. Jackson killed your father, caused your mother's death, and imprisoned Dusty for decades, just to get to you. He feared you, Nate. Feared that you'd take your rightful place. He destroyed your whole family for his own evil gain. His death is on him. If he had accepted you, loved you, helped you grow into your role as an uncle should, he would be alive."

"But..."

Her fingers pressed against his lips. "If you weren't who and what you are, Nate, I would be dead, now. The former clowder Queen would own the ranch. Ophelia would never have been born." A soft breeze from the window stroked his hair. "You are the Alpha *Were* King, but even more important, you are my everything. Don't ever, ever, say you're nothing!"

Even in the dark, her *were* vision let her see his internal struggle in the lines on his face. She cupped his face in her palm. "Curtis and Cynthia are grateful you came into their lives. Eli loves you as if you were blood. You've no idea how much everyone loves you. Supports you. Believes in you. Depends on you. Nate, you are our Alpha. Our protector." When he started to shake his head, she caught his face with both hands. "Our King."

Janelle smiled when he stilled and searched her eyes. He released a soft sigh and bowed his head. "I've been a soldier or a cop half my life, but my goal was always to save lives. I never killed if I could prevent it. I just don't know how much more killing I can..."

"Among *were*, you can offer. If blind pride and arrogance cause an Alpha to challenge, after you win the battle, you can give them the opportunity to submit. Whether they accept that opportunity is up to them. For all of us, you must be *Were* King. Lycos knows this. It's why you don't second guess yourself during battle."

"Lycos killed him. Maybe if... It's just so...different. My life has been saving people. Helping people. Lycos..." Nate shook his head.

"Did you ever have to kill on the job?"

He blinked at her, then gave her a reluctant nod.

"And you were sent for debriefing or counseling to help you deal with it, right?"

Another nod.

"So, what makes you think you don't need that now? You've been hit with a lot in the last few months." She moved to sit beside him on the bed. "Don't get lost in your head, Nate. Talk to me. Talk to your dad. Talk to Dusty, Eli, Jonathan, or Daryll. Maybe even Don. Let us help you sort through this."

A shudder went through his large frame, then he relaxed and gave her a weak smile. "Thanks, Janelle. It's just that...I never felt like anything special. In battle, I act. It just happens. But then later, I..."

"Second guess every move?"

"Yeah. I can't help but wonder if I could've done something that would've... I don't know. Made a difference? Convinced him to..." He shook his head, eyes closed, then tapped his head. "I know, in here, that I did the best I could, but..." He placed his open palm against his chest. "In here, it hurts. It feels like I didn't do enough. Like I failed, somehow."

"Maybe that's what makes you a good king. Caring so much. About everyone." She took a deep breath and let it out. "Jackson never worried about anyone but himself. From what I saw of him, neither did Ajoni. The *were* deserve a king who cares about them, and not just his own gain. That king is you."

Nate bit his lip, his face pensive, eyes searching her own. "You really think so?"

"Yes. I do. And I think the other *were* will agree with me. Especially after they get to know you." She stroked his back. "Come back to bed. You need more sleep. You can talk with Curtis or one of the others who survived combat, tomorrow. They can help you with this."

He nodded. She moved to the other side of the bed. Once he settled his head on his pillow, Janelle stretched out, rolled, and placed her head on his shoulder. He kissed her hair. "Thank you."

Her hand patted his chest. "Go to sleep, Nate." She was beginning to think he wouldn't sleep when she finally felt his body relax, heard his breathing soften. He mumbled something she didn't catch, pulled her tighter against his side, then soft snores filled the room.

A light night breeze ruffled the curtains. Her arm tingled from laying on it so long, but she didn't want to chance waking him. His role was Royal *Were* King, protector of all, *were* and human. Hers was to protect and care for him. Eventually, the sun peeked over the low hills surrounding the ranch, casting morning light through the window. Crickets and birds woke and serenaded the ranch.

In her crib, Ophelia whimpered. Careful not to jostle Nate, Janelle slipped out of his arms and walked to her daughter. After a quick diaper change, Ophelia gurgled her delight at being comfortable. Janelle picked her up and cradled the infant in her arms. "Shhh. Don't wake Daddy. Let's go downstairs and have some breakfast." With a final glance at Nate, Janelle tiptoed across the room and quietly shut the door behind her.

Chapter 9

Nate stepped off the front porch and looked around. Since their guests from yesterday returned to the inn, life was back to normal. So far, Lycos was quiet. *Wonder how long that'll last?*

Ben ran through the field, the teens running in training formation behind him. Each teen wore a sixty-pound backpack. The children played in the compound yard, chasing each other and squealing with laughter and joy. Nate closed his eyes, enjoying the morning sunshine and the normal daily sounds around him.

Cynthia's soft voice broke into his thoughts. "Morning, Son."

Smiling, Nate turned and caught his mother in a hug, lifting her off her feet. "Morning, Mom." Somehow, they were even closer after the adoption of his foster parents.

Cynthia laughed, her hand on her head to keep her sun hat from flying off. "You seem to be in a better mood, today."

"I suppose." Nate set her down and bent to see her face beneath the floppy brim of her straw hat. "Dad in his office?"

"He is. He and Don had some things to do, today." She patted his arm. "Have you had coffee?"

Nate nodded. "But there's plenty left if you want some. Janelle is feeding Ophelia in the kitchen."

"Good. I wanted to ask her about shopping for Ophelia. She's about grown out of all her clothes."

"Shopping? Now?"

She tilted her head and studied him like she did when he was a teen and trying to keep secrets. "Something wrong with now?"

Biting his bottom lip, Nate finally shook his head. "Not if you take Jonathan and Ben with you. If Ophelia goes, Snarl goes, too."

"Why?"

"It's just...well, until this coronation stuff is over with, I don't like the idea of my favorite ladies being unguarded."

"You think someone would try to hurt us? Ferocious werewolves like us?"

Nate snickered. "I don't know, Mom. I just want to make sure nothing happens to any of you."

A smile softened her face. "Then we'll just stay here and do our shopping online. Better?"

"Thanks. I wouldn't get much done if I was worried about you three." Nate gave her a quick peck on the cheek, then released her. "The laptop is on my desk. Feel free to use it."

"We will." Cynthia grinned. "And your credit card?"

Nate laughed. "I get it. You shop and I pay."

"Turnabout is fair play. It's not been that many years since I worried about my card balance when you boys went for school clothes."

He took a step toward the building his dad, Major Thomas, renovated for use as his office and barracks for the men General Brighton assigned to him. Glancing back at his mom, he grinned. "Spend whatever you want. My card is in the top right desk drawer."

Cynthia pretended to pout. "Now I'll feel guilty if I

spend too much."

"Good. My plan is working." Nate avoided the swat she aimed at his behind and chuckled at her. It was good to feel like himself again. While she walked up the steps to the front door, he hurried to the Marine Shack. Before the massacre, the building was used as a schoolhouse. After that, the building gave the surviving kids nightmares, so Nate designated the building for use as a barracks and office for the Marines General Brighton, Nate's former Marine Special Forces commander, insisted be stationed on the ranch. A brief memory of the smell of blood washed over him when he opened the door. Nate shuddered and pushed thoughts of the ranch massacre from his mind.

Major Curtis Thomas, Lieutenant Donald Dunn, and two privates bent over a map spread on the major's desk. One of the soldiers had a finger pointed at the map, moving it as he spoke. "Here, here, and here, Sir. We'll have the surveillance grid complete this afternoon."

"Surveillance?"

The Major, his dad, looked up and smiled. "Morning, Son." Dismissing the two privates, he motioned for Nate to come closer. "I got to thinking yesterday about all the cameras and spy equipment we confiscated from Zoe's aunt. With all that is going on these days, I thought we might set up a perimeter with the cameras."

Nate glanced at the map his dad motioned toward. "That's a map of the ranch."

"It was in the stuff Peyton took from Gisele's garage. I had the men install surveillance cameras at each point I've marked on the map." His finger pointed toward each red circle. "They're outside the normal run areas for the pack, but inside the ranch fence. If anyone sneaks on the ranch, we'll see them."

"How are they monitored?"

"I set up a control room in the smallest classroom." Curtis led Nate down the hall to a small room. Six folding tables lined the walls, two computers sitting on each table. On the center table, a 42" computer monitor showed a dozen small squares holding what each of the smaller screens around the room displayed, all images from cameras in the woods along the ranch fence line. Another map of the ranch hung on the wall above the main monitor, red lines breaking the property into sections marked A through F.

With an approving nod, Nate glanced at each monitor and studied the scene it showed, then walked to the large monitor on the center table. The only chair in the room was placed in front of the main monitor. A different private sat there, watching the screen.

"Anything, yet, O'Reilly?"

"No, Sir. Just trees, birds, and animals, so far."

"Good." Curtis turned to Nate. "Since the equipment was here, I thought it would be good to use it."

"All of this was Gisele's?"

"Janelle said it was all purchased with the funds Gisele stole from pack accounts. So, technically, it's yours."

Nate moved around the room, studying the placement of the cameras. "This is a great idea. After the last attack, I'll sleep better knowing this is here."

"So, will I." Curtis motioned toward the door. "I was just about to break for some coffee. Join me?"

"Sure."

"Major?"

His dad turned toward the soldier at the desk. "Yes?"

"There's someone on the ranch."

Nate whirled and took a step toward the screen. A man dressed in a Huntsman's camouflage uniform leaned against a tree, peering around. After a brief hesitation, he jogged to another tree. Nate studied the other camera images. "He's alone?"

"Yes, Sir. The cameras haven't caught anyone else."

The face was new to Nate. "Where is that camera?"

"In Section E, Sir." The soldier pointed at the map on the wall. "North corner."

The man left the small square on the screen. A few seconds later, he reappeared in a different area of the screen. "Where's he headed?"

"Toward the compound, Sir." The soldier looked up at Nate. "If he keeps moving at that pace, he'll be at the compound edge in fifteen minutes."

Nate pulled his phone from his pocket and called Ben. When the werepanther answered, he spoke a few terse orders, then turned to watch the screens. Ben and the teens ran into one of the screen images. Hiding their backpacks in the brush, the teens shifted into their respective animals. After the training Nate insisted be given to them, their clothes shifted with them, eliminating the need to disrobe before shifting. The panthers scaled the trees to hide, while the wolves hid beneath the brush and briars. In seconds, the *were* were completely hidden from sight. Nate nodded approval.

Branches swayed gently in the Texas breeze. Nothing

else moved. *Wonder if he'll notice the small animals and birds have gone away?* With *were* around, animals concealed themselves to escape the predators around them.

"There." The soldier pointed at a small section of the screen. "He'll be surrounded when he reaches the center of that clearing."

The man on the screen tested each step before moving forward. A hunter's walk. Quiet and deadly. His hand rested on the snap of his holster, ready to pop it open and grasp the grip. Determination etched his face. And fear. Whatever he was doing on the ranch, he was terrified.

Chapter 10

Colonel Lee Hill leaned against a huge live oak tree. The wind rustled leaves on the trees. Something was different. Wrong. He looked around but couldn't see anything out of the ordinary. Just trees and scrub brush and weeds, but it was so quiet. *That's it.* The birds stopped singing. None of the small animals he'd heard earlier were scurrying in the woods. Taking a deep breath, trying to work up his courage, he took another step, then froze. A wolf stepped out of the brush beneath the trees and looked at him.

Larger than a normal wolf by at least a hundred pounds, it didn't move. Just looked at him. One-by-one, another six wolves stepped out of the brush. Hand on his holster's snap, Lee looked from one to the other without moving anything but his eyes.

Then he heard a soft thump behind him. Turning ever so slowly, making no sudden moves, he caught his breath when he saw a huge black panther padding toward him. The cat's head was level with his shoulder. Lee swallowed hard. Wolves he knew of, but panthers? More panthers dropped from trees. *What are panthers doing here? They can't be shifters like the wolves. Can they?*

The first panther came closer. Lee took a step back. A soft growl behind him stopped him. The animals, wolves, bears, and panthers on every side, moved closer. Wolves he knew. He turned to the wolf and raised his hands.

"If you...if you're a werewolf, I surrender." He thought the quiver in his voice was understandable.

In the space of a blink, the wolf became a teenager. "What do you want?"

Lee studied the torn jeans and t-shirt the boy wore. Since when could werewolves change form wearing clothes? "I..." He swallowed. He was not going to tell them the Triumvirate sent him. Licking his lips, he muttered, "I'm looking for my girlfriend."

"You're what?"

"Girlfriend. Paige. Paige Marston?"

The teen tilted his head and looked at him for a moment, then glanced past Lee. Lee turned to see a man standing behind him. With a wave at the *were* animals, he ordered, "You guys get back to your run. Meet me at the picnic shelter when you're done."

The teen shifted back to a wolf. Wolves, panthers, and bears melted into the shadows beneath the brush. The man motioned toward the gun on Lee's hip. "Take that out, slow, and lay it on the ground."

Lee swallowed. He unsnapped his holster, caught the grip in two fingers, pulled it out, then bent and put the gun on the ground. Hands high, he stood, his eyes never leaving the panther man. "Do you know Paige?"

"She's at the main house." He walked forward until his boot was beside the pistol. "Move back."

Lee swallowed, took five steps back. "You're a..."

"Panther. Yes, I am." His eyes never leaving Lee's face, the man squatted and picked up the gun.

Lee searched his face. "Is Paige okay? I mean, you guys didn't..."

"Eat her? Make her one of us?" He stood and shook his head, a grin on his lips. "No, we didn't."

44

"Can I see her?"

"Probably. After Nate talks with you."

"Nate?"

"The Alpha."

"Alpha? I thought...I didn't think the alpha's name was Nate. I thought it was Hynson. Something Hynson."

"It was. Hynson died."

"Nate killed him?"

The man frowned. "No. Nate didn't kill him." He motioned for Lee to walk ahead of him. "Let's go."

Lee tried, but his feet seemed stuck to the ground. The man took his arm and shoved him forward. He stumbled a bit, then caught his balance. Now that he was moving, his feet remembered how to walk.

They walked through the trees for a few minutes, then the trees opened into a clearing with houses on every side. Glancing around, Lee saw a large fish tank, a picnic shelter, and several outbuildings. In the compound center, dozens of children played in the yard. Beyond the kids, the main house stood two stories tall.

Lee wondered if they were going to the house, but the panther turned and led him to a smaller building that reminded Lee of a schoolhouse. The panther man pulled open a door and shoved Lee inside. Lee staggered, then caught himself. He blinked as his eyes adjusted to the lower light inside. Four men turned to look at him. He was facing...soldiers? "Marines."

The Marine major nodded. "Observant, aren't you?"

"What are Marines doing here?"

"Outpost." The major frowned. "What are you doing here?"

Lee swallowed but didn't answer.

A man in jeans and a navy t-shirt took a step forward, arms crossed over his chest. "What are you doing here?"

The panther man behind him spoke up. "Says he's here for Paige."

The man in the t-shirt frowned. "Paige Marston? Why?"

"Says she's his girlfriend, Nate."

Lee's gaze was searching the room, looking for escape routes until the panther man called the guy in jeans Nate. His eyes snapped to the Alpha.

Nate's face was emotionless. "Hmm. Wonder why she didn't mention him?" He turned to one of the soldiers. "Don, call the house. Have them send Paige, Phillip, and Peyton."

Startled, Lee gasped. "Peyton's here? And Phillip?"

Nate looked at Lee, eyebrows low on his forehead. "They are. You know them?"

"Umm. Yeah."

"So, I'm assuming they know you?"

Lee nodded but didn't speak.

Don picked up the phone. After a few terse words, he disconnected the call. "They're on the way, Nate."

So, this is the Alpha. Lee looked closer. Surely, the Marines wouldn't let the Alpha just kill him. Then again, after a glance at the blank faces of the uniformed men, Lee was unsure they would even try to stop the Alpha if he decided to do just that.

Chapter 11

Paige walked with Phillip and her dad to the Marine Shack. Don called and ordered them to come to the building but didn't say why. She twisted the end of her ponytail around her fingers and chewed her bottom lip. She glanced at her dad. "Are we in trouble?"

Peyton Marston shrugged. "Not that I know of. I don't know any more than you do." He stepped forward and opened the door for Paige and Phillip to precede him into the building. "In you go, kids."

At twenty-two years old, and Phillip nineteen, Paige wondered how he could consider them kids, anymore. She shrugged and grinned. He would probably always call them kids.

Paige stepped inside, blinking until her eyes adjusted to the difference in the lighting. Four Marines in uniform stood behind Nate. Ben stood beside a man in Huntsmen uniform. She glanced at his face, then gaped at him. "Colonel? Lee? What are you doing here?"

Nate took a step toward her. "Says he's your boyfriend."

Paige leaned back, chin tucked, her eyes wide. She shook her head once, then glared at Lee. "My what?"

Lee swallowed. "We dated."

"Two years ago!" Paige marched to him, poked his chest with her forefinger. "What are you talking about?"

Lee opened his mouth to speak, but Peyton beat him to it. "What do you mean calling my daughter your girlfriend, young man? You've been running around with other girls!"

Panic entering his face, Lee looked from Peyton to Paige. "Paige, I...I missed you."

Nate cleared his throat. "So, he's not your boyfriend?"

Missed me? Paige opened her mouth and took a breath, but no words came out.

"Well?"

The growl in Nate's voice frightened her. "Nate, I...well, we did date, but that's been a while back, and I..." She shook her head and turned to Lee. "Why did you come here?"

"You didn't come back." Lee shrugged. He squirmed under her gaze. "I was afraid something happened to you."

Paige took a deep breath and let out a long sigh. She studied his face for a moment, then looked at Nate. "May I talk with him alone?"

Nate sucked air between his teeth. Behind him, the phone shrilled.

Don answered it, then covered it with his hand. "The Kanha and Siberia Ambush Queens, and the Gir Forest Pride King are checking in, Nate."

Nate's eyes briefly glowed turquoise. His shoulders tightened. He shuddered, then relaxed, sighed and looked at Paige. "I don't have time to deal with your friend right now." He glanced at Peyton. "Peyton, he's in your custody. Find out why he's here. And get that ring off him." He walked toward the door.

Paige raised a finger in the air. "Um, Nate? Maybe we should leave it on for a while."

Nate stopped and looked back over his shoulder at her.

48

"Why?"

The intensity of his gaze sent shivers down her back. *Nate's not happy. And when Nate's not happy...* The last few days, Nate seemed stressed. Paige cleared her throat. "While he wears it, they'll think he's still working for them. We take it off, they'll think we killed him."

Nate pursed his lips and raised an eyebrow at Lee. Frowning, he nodded. "For now, then." He looked past Paige and Peyton to the major. "Let Jonathan know if you need more equipment. This surveillance idea of yours is great."

The major gave the Alpha a single nod. Nate hurried out, the door slamming behind him. Paige stared at the door, then turned to face Lee and groaned. "Dad, is it okay if I take Lee to the gazebo for a chat?"

Peyton nodded permission. "We'll be close enough to hear if you shout."

"Thanks, Dad."

*****

Shoulders hunched, hands jammed deep in his front pockets, Lee glanced at Paige as she walked ahead of him. Back stiff, arms straight, and hands clenched tight at her side, she led him to a two-story gazebo on the other side of the picnic pavilion.

She pointed at the table beneath the second story gazebo platform.

"Sit down."

Lee pulled his hands from his pockets and sat. He looked up at her, his hands dangling between his knees.

"Why are you so mad, Paige?"

She huffed at him. "Why did you lie? Since when are you my boyfriend?"

He looked down at his hands. "I would be if you weren't so stubborn."

"What?"

He refused to look up. "You're the one that broke it off."

"You took Stacy Ann on a date!"

"It wasn't a date. I told you that, already."

She stomped her foot on the grass. "Fine. Why are you here?"

"You didn't come back. I thought you died."

"So, you what? Came to avenge me?"

He shrugged. "Maybe."

"Ugh!" Paige stepped on the picnic table bench next to his left thigh, pivoted, and sat on the table he leaned against. "Would you look at me?"

He twisted at the waist and raised his gaze to her. Sunlight cast golden sparkles in her hair. She was still the most beautiful girl he'd ever seen. In her eyes, he saw anger. And fear. While she searched his face, he studied her expression. Lee turned, straddled the bench, one leg under the table, and put his left hand on her thigh. "What are you afraid of, Paige?"

She blinked back tears and caught his left hand in both hers. "I have to know, Lee. Did you come on your own, or did the Triumvirate send you?"

"Does it matter?"

"It does." She chewed her bottom lip. "It matters to me. And to them."

50

"And if they sent me?"

"You have to tell Nate."

Lee huffed. "Yeah, like that'll happen."

"I'm serious, Lee. You don't know what's really going on. Nate and the others...they're the good guys."

Lee's jaw ticked, aware the emotions on his face slid away. He tilted his head and looked at Paige. "What did they do to you?"

"Nothing!"

"Then why did you change sides?"

Paige dropped his hand as if it burned her. "Why are you really here?"

"To get you out of here, if I can."

"Is that all?"

When he didn't answer, she stood, jumped to the ground, and turned to study his face. "If I can't trust you...if you don't tell me the truth, I can't help you. As far as I know, Nate doesn't kill trespassers. Not like Hynson did, but he won't just let you go, either."

"Tell me what happened."

"Zoe nearly killed my dad. Nate saved him."

"How?" She didn't answer, but there was only one way a werewolf could 'save' someone who was dying. He swallowed hard. "Nate changed him?" Lee frowned, closed his eyes, and bowed his head. "You know he has to die, right?"

Her palm smacked the side of his head.

"Ow!" Hand on his throbbing ear, he spun to get both feet on the same side of the bench, then surged to his feet and stood glaring at Paige. "What did you do that for?"

"You're not listening!"

"What? You said your dad's a werewolf!"

"I said Nate saved him!"

Lee fought the grin that tried to form on his lips when she glared at him. He'd almost forgotten how cute she was when she was angry. "And?"

"I also said Nate and the others here are the good guys. The Triumvirate is evil, Lee!"

The urge to grin went away. "Evil how?"

"You won't believe me." She shook her head. "I didn't believe it, either, when I was first told."

"Told what?"

"The Triumvirate are vampires. They only want to kill the *were*, because while the *were* live, they can't enslave humans."

Of all the stupid... "Vampires."

"Yes, vampires."

Lee dropped to the bench and looked up at her. Shaking his head, he blew out a long breath, then put his elbows on his knees and his face in his hands. "They've brainwashed you."

"No." Her soft voice brought his gaze back to her face. "No, the Triumvirate have brainwashed generations of Huntsmen." She swallowed. "When was the last time you saw Stacy Ann?"

"What?"

"Stacy Ann. When did you see her last?"

"I don't know." Confused, Lee shook his head. "Not long before you disappeared, why?"

"She and Mark tried to run away. The Triumvirate sent a team after them. When the team brought them back, they took his ring from him. Killed him."

He shook his head. "They wouldn't do that."

"They did. And then they fed off Stacy until she died. They drank all her blood." A tear slipped down her face. "Zoe saw it all, Lee. They killed them both, then put a geas on Zoe to come after me and kill me, Philip, and Dad."

He moaned, his head still shaking left to right. *That can't be right. It can't!* "Paige..."

"She almost succeeded, Lee. Nate and his people saved us. They took the geas from her. Zoe was injured, so they took her to the hospital for treatment. One of the nurses was a Huntsman. She tried to kill Zoe. If not for Daryll, she would have." Paige touched his face, her soft fingers brushing his late day stubble. "You have to tell us why you're here. Please, Lee."

Lee closed his eyes for a moment, then pressed his hand to the back of hers where she still cupped his face in her palm. "So, Zoe's a wolf, too?"

Her sigh was so heartfelt it pained him. "No, she's not." She swallowed and blinked. "She's a...a bear."

"A bear." Lee studied Paige's face and eyes. *She believes this stuff!*

"Yes, a bear. Daryll changed her when she was mortally wounded during the last attack."

"Daryll. The guy that took her to a hospital. He's a bear. A werebear."

Paige nodded. "A bear shifter."

"And the Triumvirate are evil vampires." His deadpan delivery brought anger to her eyes.

"It's true, Lee! I promise."

"Prove what you just told me, and I'll do whatever you

want me to. But, Paige." The expression in her eyes tied his stomach in knots. *Who knows? If there are werepanthers, maybe there are werebears. And vampires, too. Too much. It's too much!* The memory of glowing, sickly whitish yellow eyes staring at him swept into his mind. He swallowed and took her hands in his. "If you can't prove it, your dad has to die. And Zoe, too."

Chapter 12

During the short trip to Hallettsville, Snarl watched the other vehicles on the road. If the Huntsmen had any idea what Nate was doing, an attack was imminent. While Jonathan drove the SUV, Nate sat in the back working with his tablet. After the fiasco with Ajoni, Nate decided he would show up each time one of the Alphas, Kings, or Queens checked into the inn. Snarl agreed. Stopping trouble before it started was a good plan.

Snarl and Jonathan followed Nate into the inn. Zoe waved and motioned toward the breakfast area where low murmured conversation filled the air. The new groups were gathered around three tables drinking coffee. Donuts and pastries were available on the banquet table, but few of the guests partook from the offered treats.

Two steps behind Nate, Snarl walked past the low half-wall separating the foyer and check-in desk from the dining area, stepped to the right and stopped, while Jonathan stepped to the left. A quick survey identified the two ambush Queens and the pride King. Snarl's eyes narrowed, but he kept his frown off his face. The man he studied wasn't King Lamor, though the resemblance to his old friend was striking. His wolf sniffed, then yipped happily in Snarl's mind. *Prince Hansh!* Conversation stopped and all turned their gazes to Nate. Curiosity filled their faces. Snarl released a quiet sigh of relief. Though tension was clear, no animosity filled the room.

Nate cleared his throat. "Good afternoon. I'm Nate Rollins, the Alpha for the Texas Ranch Wolf Pack." From the corner of his eye, Snarl watched Nate wave a hand at Jonathan but kept his gaze on the Alpha's guests. "This is Jonathan Dyers, my Beta. If you need anything or have any problems while you are here, see Jonathan. The front desk will have his phone number for you. He will arrange reimbursement for your travel expenses, too."

The copper embroidery on Prince Hansh's teal silk kurta glimmered in the low light when he leaned forward. Face blank, Snarl studied the man. Hansh wasn't the young cub he was the last time Snarl saw him.

"I am Hansh, Prince of the Gir Forest Pride. You are the reason we are here?"

Nate nodded. "I am."

"And you think you should be *Were* King? Tell us why."

Nate's shoulders and back stiffened, then slowly relaxed. Snarl tensed. Nate never let his feelings show like that. He must still be having trouble controlling Lycos. Nate gave the prince a slight bow. "I am a wolf of Royal Descent. With permission of the Ancients, I bear four of the five Royal medallions. The Ancients charge me to protect all *were* and all humans. I can best do that if I am *Were* King."

Snarl turned his gaze on the tiger and lion shifters as they exchanged glances. On the highway outside the inn, eighteen-wheelers rumbled, barely heard inside. The air conditioner started humming in the background. Hansh stood up, arrogance in his stance. "You can prove you have the medallions?"

"I can, but not here. This area is not private enough. We can either adjourn to a meeting room, or I'll have

Jonathan call SUVs to transport us all to the ranch. Your choice."

Hansh leaned his head back, chin tilted up, and raised an eyebrow. "This place is not safe?" Snarl almost grinned. Hansh reminded him so much of his father.

"Safe, yes, as much as we can make it, but not secure from surprise human visits. At any time, someone could walk in the front door." Nate tilted his head. "They would be told all the rooms are reserved, so they would not stay. But they could come in."

A woman cleared her throat. Her gold-flecked eyes matched the red, gold embroidered sari draped over her slight form. "I am Arkasha, Queen of the Kanha Ambush. Seringi has informed us that you are willing to accept any Alpha challenge and have already won the Kingship of the Serengeti Pride."

"King Ajoni challenged. I won. Seringi is temporary Alpha King to the Serengeti Pride. If he can hold the position when he returns home, Seringi is their king."

Hansh's forehead lowered over his gold eyes. "Why? You earned the right to be their king."

"To meet my charge, I must be *Were* King, King of all *Were*. I will not be able to administer the daily needs of a people on the other side of the world while attending to the *Were* King's duties." Nate's sigh was faint, almost inaudible. "There's more. Maybe your histories mention that the last time *were* tried to coronate a *Were* King, Huntsmen attacked. Most of the attendees at the coronation died."

The men and women glanced at each other. The second Queen nodded. Snarl studied her black silk gown embroidered with burgundy roses. "I am Gavrilla, Queen of the Siberian Ambush. This information is in our history. Is there reason to believe this is a danger now?"

Nate gave them a short nod. "There is. We've had several problems with Huntsmen. This is the reason I'm calling each group of *were* to meet with me before the coronation festivities. We have someone with us who was present at the doomed coronation your histories mention. It is his belief that the reason the *were* failed was they were too busy arguing who would be king to properly defend against a common enemy."

Gavrilla laughed. "That occurred over six hundred years ago."

"It's true, though. May I introduce to you, Snarl, also known as Thorkell Ericsson, grandson of Erik the Red, the last *Were* King." Nate turned to his left and waved his hand toward Snarl. "Snarl is my resource for *were* history, my friend, advisor, and self-proclaimed bodyguard."

Snarl stepped forward and gave a slight bow to the group. Wide-eyed, Hansh stared at Snarl. He sniffed, then grinned and bowed his head. "Greetings, Old One."

Snarl gave the Gir Forest Pride Prince a formal bow. "Your Highness. It is good to see you again."

Nate quirked an eyebrow at Snarl, then turned his gaze to Hansh. "You've met, then."

Hansh nodded and grinned. "Kell was a guest of the Pride for many years when I was a cub. He was an advisor to my father." The Pride Prince turned to the two Queens. "If Kell says he was there, he was there. He was an old man when my grandfather was born." Hansh glanced again at Snarl. "Though you don't look so old, now, as you once did, my friend."

Snarl chuckled. "I started using a glamour during the eleventh-century wars in Europe." He raised one shoulder and let it drop. "I had no desire to be conscripted into any human army. Only women, very old men, and very young children were exempt. In this country, at least for now, it is not a concern. These days, I go by Snarl."

The fierce tension in the room faded into alertness. Gavrilla stood up, her silk skirts rustling, her chair sliding silently on the carpet. "I propose we adjourn to the ranch for a demonstration of your medallions' power."

Nate glanced at Hansh and Arkasha. They both nodded. Arkasha stood to join the others.

"Okay." Nate turned to Jonathan. "Have three SUVs brought in for them."

Jonathan pulled out his phone. "They're already here, Nate. I have the drivers assigned rooms here for the duration of the visits." When Nate nodded approval, Jonathan walked toward the door while he dialed.

The desk phone rang, and Zoe answered it speaking in quiet tones. She hung up the phone and walked to the breakfast area. "Nate?"

He turned, an eyebrow raised. "Zoe?"

"That was Dusty. The Borneo Leap Patriarch and the Tennessee Highland Rim Queen landed nearly two hours ago. They'll be here sometime in the next half hour."

"Thanks, Zoe. Is Daryll here?"

When she nodded, Nate smiled. "Good. Call Dusty back and have him drive directly to the ranch. Then call Janelle and tell her to have Reese and Bobby start up the barbeque pits."

He thought for a moment, then added. "Have one of the others take over the desk, and you and Daryll go to the meat market. Purchase all the steaks and hamburger they have. We'll have steaks for our guests and burgers for the kids. Oh, and tell Janelle to start baked potatoes and have the kids make some ice cream, too."

"Yes, Sir." She returned to the desk and started making calls.

Ice cream. Snarl snickered and stood aside to let Nate walk out ahead of him. *The Alpha sure likes homemade ice cream.*

Chapter 13

Janelle looked out the office window at the ranch. She set Ophelia's juice bottle on the window sill, then lifted the baby to her shoulder to burp her. Three SUVs pulled into the parking area. Passengers dressed in fashions from foreign countries departed the vehicles. The small bus used to transport arrivals from the airport to the inn pulled in and parked at the end of the line of SUVs. After most of the passengers debarked, Nate stepped out of the first SUV. He spoke to their guests, then led them toward the house.

Snagging the almost empty bottle, Janelle moved to the office door, opened it, and leaned out. "Mom? Cynthia?"

After a moment, Cynthia stuck her head out of the nursery. "Morning, Janelle. I finished putting away Ophelia's laundry. Need something?"

Janelle nodded. "Nate is back, and he has a crowd with him. Will you take Ophelia for a while?"

Cynthia's blue eyes brightened. "Of course." With three quick steps, Cynthia reached for her granddaughter. "Come to Grandma, sweet girl!"

Ophelia gurgled at her grandmother, and Cynthia laughed. "She doesn't look ready for a nap to me."

A soft smile touched Janelle's lips. "I'm afraid not. She slept most of the morning."

The front door opened on the first floor. Multiple footsteps started up the stairs. Cynthia slipped into the nursery and shut the door without a sound. Janelle walked back to the window and glanced toward the picnic shelter. Reese and Bobby watched flames shooting up from the pits, while a dozen teens cranked old-fashioned ice cream makers. Two large pots, both full of potatoes, boiled on the gas grill next to the pits. There wasn't enough time to let them bake, so she decided to use an old restaurant trick to get them done. Satisfied she would have everything ready when Zoe and Daryll showed up with the steaks, she nodded, then moved to stand behind her chair.

The door opened. Nate walked through, Snarl behind him, then people unknown to Janelle. Three women, a man younger than Janelle expected, and an older man entered the office. Each was followed by a group of three to six retainers. Nate motioned for them to join him at the conference table. The five leaders sat down, their retainers standing against the wall behind them.

When he reached Janelle, Nate's hand briefly clasped her fingers. He gave her an absent smile, then turned to face his visitors. "Welcome to Texas Ranch Wolf Pack Headquarters. For those who have not met me, I am Nate Rollins, Pack Alpha." He nodded toward Janelle. "This is my mate, Queen, and Pack Mother, Janelle."

Janelle's curious gaze traveled to each of the five guests. She smiled. "Welcome to our home."

Nate pulled out Janelle's chair. She sat and he scooted her chair to the table. His hand caressed her shoulder briefly, then he sat beside her. Janelle glanced at the worry lines on Nate's forehead. With effort, she managed to keep concern from her expression. Jonathan walked along the wall and stood in his place behind Nate's right shoulder.

Nadrai squirmed, restless in Janelle's mind. Keeping her face emotionless, Janelle sent a query to Nadrai. *Something wrong?*

Koreth and Nate are stressed. While considering Nadrai's thought, Janelle glanced at Nate. The muscle in his jaw ticked. Janelle sent a thought to Koreth. His refusal to answer left her blinking.

The oldest of their guests tapped twice on the table, then leaned forward. "I am Izzat, Patriarch of the Borneo Leap. Who are you to demand we attend you?"

He is a clouded leopard. Janelle sent Nadrai thanks for the identification.

At her shoulder, Nate stiffened. Janelle glanced at him and bit her lip when she saw the anger in his eyes. Slowly, he stood to his full height. He was trembling as if he could barely hold his temper. "I am he who will be your King. Take care with your tone."

At Nate's formal words, everything seemed to slow. The Borneo Patriarch's chair crashed to the floor. His retainers stepped close behind him. He jutted his chin toward Nate. "That is yet to be decided, Pup."

Nate's head dropped back, and he shimmered into Lycos. Janelle jumped to her feet and caught his arm. "Nate...Lycos, there is no challenge here. No need to fight."

"You will not interfere, Woman!"

"Nate..."

Without looking her way, Lycos caught her left shoulder in his claws. Pain knifed into her shoulder as his claws tore through her blouse and into her flesh. Gasping, she tried to pull away. Lycos threw her across the table.

Janelle crashed into one of the Queens, then rolled back onto the table. Scrambling to her knees, right hand pressed against her bleeding shoulder, Janelle faced Lycos. "Nate, no!"

Lycos shuddered, his eyes changing from shining turquoise to Nate's familiar grey, then back to turquoise. "You will not command me!"

With a roar, he leaned across the table, his claws reaching for her arm. Janelle backed away, then stopped as Lycos froze. His tall form shuddered, the color of his eyes flickering from turquoise to grey, and then back again. She moved between the two Queens, turned, and swung her feet over the edge of the table. Their visitors shoved away from the table, their retinue surrounding them.

Standing, she whipped around to face Nate. He shimmered, as if returning to his human form, then Lycos threw his head back and roared so loud everyone in the room covered their ears with their hands. The glow faded. He shimmered again and became Nate. Gasping, he staggered back, his gaze on Janelle.

"Are you hurt?" His whispered question seemed loud in the silence. Then the shimmer of change started again. *Run!* Nadrai shouted in her mind. *Run, now!*

As if from a great distance, she heard Koreth's mental roar. *Run, Janelle! We can't hold Lycos!*

Lycos bellowed and jumped up on the table toward Janelle. Squealing, Janelle threw open the door and ran, her feet pounding the stairs. Lycos crashed down the steps behind her. She hit the front screen door, thankful the wooden door wasn't closed. Jumping off the front porch, she took three steps, then screamed when Lycos' claws caught her. He raised his other arm, his three-inch claws swept toward her.

"No, Lycos! I am your mate!" Her shoulder burned. Janelle closed her eyes, not wanting to see the claws strike her. When the blow she expected didn't come, she opened her eyes and blinked.

Nate stood before her, his hand on her arm, the other arm still in the air. "I'm sorry, Janelle. I would never..." Again, the air around him started to glimmer. Crying out, anger and fear in his face, Nate released Janelle, stumbled and nearly fell, then dropped to his knees when Lycos took over again.

Snarl jumped past Lycos, caught Janelle's arm, and pulled her behind him. "Stay back!"

"What's wrong with him, Snarl?"

"It's the medallions. Nate must subdue Lycos, or he will never be himself again."

"What?" Janelle shook her head, ignoring the moisture on her cheeks. "I don't understand."

Snarl kept his back to Janelle, his gaze fixed on Lycos. "It is traditional for Royal Alphas to wear only one medallion. It is forbidden to wear more than two. Each medallion increases the power of the Lycos form. The Progenitors gave Nate permission to wear four, but if it becomes powerful enough to take over, the Progenitors may need to destroy Nate and the medallions. For all our sakes."

"No!" Janelle caught Snarl's arm. "They can't!"

Lycos took a step toward Snarl. Snarl waved his hand and a glowing shield of light formed between them. "I have no desire for the medallions, Lycos, but I will remove them from the one who wears them if you do not retreat!" He spread his fingers wide with a quick snap. The light grew to a pulsing wall of blue.

Lycos' harsh, guttural voice boomed through the compound. "The bearer is weak. He wishes to give those who follow choices. It is his destiny to be *Were* King. I cannot allow one who is weak to take the throne."

"It is true the bearer will not force anyone to kneel. It is not weakness, but rather honor!"

Huge furred head shaking, Lycos took another step. "The female makes him weak!"

Arm out to keep Janelle behind him, Snarl backed up a step. "The female is his mate and mother to his pup! If you harm her, he will destroy you."

Lycos roared, took a step that shook the ground. "She makes us weak! She will die!" He took another step, stopped and shuddered. The shimmer washed over him, left Nate.

Gasping, his arms clutched over his abdomen, Nate turned a tight face to the wolf protecting his mate. "Snarl, what can I do?"

"Remove the medallions."

"I can't!"

"Then Janelle may die. You know I can't hold Lycos back for long."

Nate's gaze slipped past Snarl. He took a harsh breath through clenched teeth. "I'm sorry, Janelle." He swallowed hard, his chin trembling. "I love you beyond life!" As the shimmer started again, Nate slipped a hand inside his shirt, clasped the melded medallions, and pulled with all his strength. "Ahhh!"

His pain-filled scream caught Janelle's heart in a vise, and she sobbed. The smell of burnt flesh hit Janelle at the same time the light shimmering around Nate intensified so bright it blinded her. As quickly as it came, it was gone. Janelle blinked, took a deep breath, and gazed around the compound.

"Where is he, Snarl?" Her fingers clamped tighter on Snarl's arm. "Where's Nate?"

The wall of light Snarl conjured dissipated in the air. He turned to face Janelle. Gently, he removed his arm from her hands. His sad eyes told her more than his words. "He's gone, Janelle."

Swallowing the screams crowding her throat, Janelle took a deep breath. "He'll be back. He has to come back!" *Was that frantic voice hers?*

Snarl gave her a hesitant nod. "If he can regain control, the Progenitors will send him back. If he can't..."

Thunder crashed. Janelle's gaze snapped to the burst of light beyond Snarl. Snarl whirled and dropped into a defensive stance. The light died and Lycos stood in the center of the compound yard, a woman clutching his elbow. As soon as the light cleared, Snarl stood. Eli was no threat to Janelle.

"Renate!" Janelle sank to the grass.

Renate raced to her and dropped to her knees beside Janelle. "You're wounded! What happened? Eli said something was wrong, then left. I just barely caught his arm to come with him."

"Where's Nate?" demanded the Lycos beyond Snarl.

Janelle clutched Renate's hands and glanced up at

Lycos. "It was Lycos. He's gone. Snarl thinks the Progenitors took him."

"Why?"

Gasping, struggling to fight off sobs, Janelle shook her head. "Nate lost control of Lycos."

Eli's Lycos form shimmered into a human. He looked past Janelle to his parents behind Janelle's shoulder, bit his lip, then walked to his brother's mate. "He'll be fine, Janelle. Nate's a fighter and strong enough to win this."

With Eli's hands on her shoulders, Janelle took a deep breath. "You're right. He will. I know he will." She slowly stood and accepted the hug Eli and Renate gave her, then turned to face the men and women watching from the porch.

Flora Garrett, Queen of the clowder Nate gave refuge pushed past the Alphas standing on the porch, rushed to Janelle, and caught her hand. "He'll be back, Janelle. Nothing will keep him from you and Ophelia."

Janelle swallowed and nodded. "You're right."

Renate caught her free hand. "Let's get your shoulder tended."

Janelle blinked at Renate, eyes filled with tears she wouldn't let flow. As Renate and Flora led her toward the house, she smiled at Eli. "He'll be back." She sniffed. "In the meantime, we have guests. Eli, will you help Jonathan get things settled?"

"Of course." Eli turned to the crowd on the porch. "Is anyone else hurt?"

Taking a deep breath, Janelle let Eli take over the responsibilities of caring for her guests. She squared her shoulders, smiled at the men and women Lycos called to the ranch, and let her two friends lead her inside. Behind her, she heard Jonathan's voice.

"I am sure you are all tired and hungry," he said. "We'll feed you and take you to the inn for the night. When Nate returns, we will reconvene."

Chapter 14

Lee's face felt numb, his mouth agape. He blinked, realizing that he had been staring wide-eyed for much too long. Paige slipped her hand inside his elbow and pulled on him. He turned. Fear. Yes, there was fear in her eyes, but not the kind of terror he expected to see. In all the years he spent training as a Huntsman, he had never heard of a partially shifted wolf. No, a partially shifted *giant* wolf. He shook his head, not sure how to describe what he saw. "What was that?" he hissed.

Paige tugged again, led him to the gazebo, and pulled him up the stairs to the second floor. She sank down onto one of the four chairs arranged around a circular table. She turned to face him. "That was Lycos, Nate's third form."

"Lycos?"

"I don't understand it, but only a very few Royal wolves have the ability to change to Lycos. I don't know why." Her eyes closed, and she bowed her head. "Something's wrong. I've never seen him like that before."

"Like what?"

"Wild. He's usually so gentle. And Nate would never hurt Janelle. Never." She shook her head. "Something's wrong."

"The wolves seemed afraid of him."

"They aren't as powerful as he is. If he snaps, they can't stop him."

"What about the other one? Where did that come

from?"

"That's Eli, Nate's brother. Far as I know, he was in Arkansas until just now."

Lee wiped his face with both palms and let out an exasperated sigh. "Arkansas? Arkansas is hours away."

"Not for Lycos. He can...I don't know what to call it, but it's like teleportation. That's how Nate brought Dad here from Arkansas after Dad's patrol attacked the Ozark Pack."

Lee leaned on the railing, scanning the grounds below. No one paid them any attention. Turning back to Paige, he caught her hands in both his. "Paige, we have to go. While they're busy with whatever this is. We have to go."

"Go where?"

"Back to headquarters. We have to tell the Triumvirate about this Lycos thing." He pulled her to her feet and moved toward the stairs. "Come on."

Paige jerked her hands from his. "We can't!"

He spun to face her. "No one is watching. We can get out of here."

"You still don't believe me. If we go back, they'll kill us both!"

Lee let out an exasperated sigh. "Not that, again."

"It's true. You heard Janelle. Nate will be back as soon as he regains control over Lycos."

"That means we don't have much time!"

She took a step back, shaking her head. "I'm not going. The Triumvirate already tried to kill me, Lee. The wolves won't let you leave. If you try..." She swallowed. "I don't know what they'll do to you, but as long as you stay here, you're safe."

"Safe? As a prisoner to werewolves, werepanthers, and werebears?"

"She's right."

Lee spun to face Peyton. He hadn't seen Paige's father when he searched the grounds. Nor had he heard him come up the stairs. "You're compromised!" He stepped back. "You're a wolf!"

"I'm a wolf, and I'm no longer a Huntsman, but I'm not compromised. Not the way you mean." Peyton took a step toward Lee. "Let's go to the Marine Shack. There's something there you should see."

"What?"

"After all the commotion, Major Rollins called in the general. He'll be here by the time we get to the shack."

"What general?" Lee took another step back, then stopped. There really wasn't anywhere to go on the small second story platform.

"Someone you need to meet." Peyton turned and walked down the stairs.

Lee glanced at Paige. She was biting her lip like she always did when she was worried about something. He sighed. "Paige..."

Paige caught his hand and tugged him toward the stairs. "It'll be okay, Lee. I promise."

His reluctant feet followed her down the stairs, and he let her pull him toward the building the wolves called the Marine Shack. "Paige..."

She stopped and put one finger on his lips. Shaking her head, she gave him a grin. "No one will hurt you. Come on."

He glanced around. The teenage werewolf he met in

the woods stood below the second story platform in the gazebo. Six other teen boys stood with him. Realizing they had been waiting for him and Paige to come down, he sighed again and dropped his shoulders. "We would never have made it, would we?"

Paige shook her head. She gave him a sad smile. "No. They've been there the whole time."

"They heard?"

"They did."

"But why didn't...?"

"Why didn't they attack when we came down the stairs?" She took a deep breath and let it out in a rush. "I told you they won't hurt you. Come on. Let's go see what Dad wants to show you."

Just before they got to the shack, a military jeep roared up, tires screeching as it braked in front of the building. A tall man in a general's uniform stepped out. Without looking around, he marched to the shack and yanked the door open, slamming it behind him. Walking ahead of Paige and Lee, Peyton nodded to the man sitting behind the wheel in the jeep, then stepped past him to open the door. He motioned Paige and Lee inside, then followed them in.

As his eyes adjusted to the dimmer light, Lee saw the general turn to face the three newcomers. With a frown, the general crossed his arms over his chest and swept Lee with a sharp gaze. "And who are you?" he demanded

Reacting more to the voice of command than anything else, Lee snapped to attention. "Hill, Lee, Colonel. Huntsman Rover."

The general harrumphed and turned to the Major.

"What's going on here, Rollins?"

The Major, standing at parade rest, glanced past the general to Lee. "He was captured this morning, Sir."

"Is he the reason you called?"

"No, Sir. Nate disappeared. He lost control of Lycos and vanished." The emotional undertones in the major's voice surprised Lee.

"Are the other alphas still here?"

"Janelle invited them to stay for a meal before heading back to the inn, Sir. She insists he'll be back."

The general nodded. "I'm sure he will. He and Eli were the best men I had. It may take some time, but he'll be back." His glance went past Lee to Peyton. "You brought him here. Why?"

"He doesn't believe vampires exist, General. I was hoping you could help us prove him wrong."

Brighton's top lip lifted in a snarl. "And how do you suggest I do that?"

"I don't want you to bite him, Sir. Just show him." Peyton glanced at Lee. "Lee, this is General Brighton, Nate's Special Forces commander."

The general studied Lee for a moment, then asked, "He some value to you? He needs to know?"

"He was stationed at Huntsmen Headquarters in Oklahoma. As a Colonel, he has intel I didn't have access to. He could be a help."

Pressing his lips together, eyes narrowed, the general studied Lee, then nodded. "I suppose that makes sense." He took a step toward Lee.

Lee leaned back but otherwise didn't move. Peyton's words filtered through his mind. Turning his gaze to

Peyton, he frowned. "What are you talking about? I won't help you!"

"Look at me, Colonel." At the growl in the general's voice, Lee's gaze jumped back to him. "What he's trying to tell you is there are two kinds of vampires. Those who drink the blood of animals, and those who prefer human blood. Your Triumvirate is a branch of the V-Triumph, rogue vampires who want to kill *were,* so that they can breed humans to be food animals."

"You're wrong. The Huntsmen..."

"The Huntsmen were organized to destroy the *were*. Once they've accomplished that, the Huntsmen will be the first to feed the vampires you serve." The general stepped closer. Too close.

Lee swallowed. "I don't believe in vampires."

"Then you need to see one. Is that it?"

Suppressing the shiver trying to take over his entire body, Lee nodded. "Unless I see one."

The general's eyes glowed whitish yellow. His eye teeth elongated, extending well past the bottom of his lower lip and his face paled. "Don't tempt me, Colonel. I haven't eaten in days and you smell..." He leaned forward and sniffed the air. "You smell like food."

No longer able to control his shivers, Lee swallowed. Hard.

"There's something else you need to know about vampires, Colonel. We can control humans. I'm going to go into your mind and release the geas your Triumvirate commanders have placed on you. You will see everything I see. You will know everything I do. Your memories will come back to you. Nothing will be hidden from you. After

I'm done, we'll see what you think."

General Brighton's burning pus-yellow eyes captured Lee, held him tight. Lee gasped when the general's thoughts invaded his mind. Without conscious effort, Lee's eyes drifted shut. In his mind, he saw the general watching him, waiting for him to regain some semblance of calm. Once Lee was breathing easier, the general nodded. *Hundreds of years ago, the V-Triumph formed the Triumvirate to create the Huntsmen. They've been using you as soldiers and food the entire time.*

It was so strange to hear the general speaking when his ears heard nothing. In his mind, Lee asked, *Food?*

I can smell them on you, Colonel. You've fed them, you just don't remember. I would be surprised if all the Huntsmen haven't fed them at some point. I'm going to remove their memory block, but before I do, know this. I am not one of them. I command the Covenant. I have never, and will never, feed on humans. The Progenitors forbid it.

Progenitors?

The Ancients, rulers of our ancient home. Brighton clasped Lee's shoulder in a tight grip.

Visions started to play through his mind. Scenes from the past rushed by, showing Lee the trauma he had unknowingly lived through. Seeing the face of one of the Triumvirate commanders sneering as it came close, then feeling the pain of teeth tearing into his neck, the terrifying, yet pleasurable sensation of blood sucked into the vampire's mouth. Lee gasped, unable to control the fear that again swept through him. A hot tongue swept over his torn neck. Dizziness clouded his mind while strong hands held him steady on his feet.

Brighton dropped his hand and took a step back. Lee blinked, swallowed, and put his right hand to the left side of his neck. "I don't understand," he whispered. "How could that be real? I never had a wound like that!"

"Unless his victim is drained of all blood after he feeds, a vampire's saliva heals the wound. It leaves only the faintest of scars. Now that you know what to look for, next time you shave, you should see the scars. They're faint, but they're there."

Lee stared at him for a moment. More than anything, he never wanted to look into a mirror again. He didn't want to see proof of the memories the general released. Swallowing, he glanced at Paige. "They fed off me?" She gave him a sad nod. He took a shaky breath and bowed his head.

"Lee." Paige's soft voice pulled his gaze back to her. With trembling hands, she pushed aside the neckband of her t-shirt and tilted her head to the right. Faint scars marred the soft skin of her neck. Lee caught his breath and met her eyes.

"They fed off all of us. We just didn't remember it later. At the time it's terrifying, but they take the memory so that they can control us. And feed again." She sniffed and a tear traced her cheek. "We can't go back. We must stop them before they destroy all our families and friends. All humans."

Lee watched the tear slip down her cheek. He glanced again at the faint scars on her neck. Explosive anger surged through him, destroying the fear he remembered. He turned and looked at the general. "You're not like them?"

"No. I work to stop them. We all do."

Lee nodded. "I'll help you." He looked at Paige, then reached up to wipe the tear from her face. "I'll do anything to keep them from doing that to you again."

Chapter 15

Humid air brushed against Nate's skin as clouds whirled against him. Something he couldn't see touched his face, then a long, wet tongue licked him from chin to ear, followed by a soft whine. *Koreth*. The wolf's comforting presence settled him. Nate blinked and turned to look around the room. Wispy white curtains billowed at the window, glowing with light from outside. Blank white walls surrounded him, a white featureless ceiling above him. *Why am I back in the Judgement Tower?*

Koreth whined and Nate turned to see the wolf beside him, his head tilted, and tongue hanging out. *You must regain control.*

Control?

Control of Lycos. You were judged worthy of Lycos' power. But to keep it, you must have control.

Nate blinked. He slowly sat up and looked around. *Déjà vu. Been here, done this*. Everything was still white. And there were still no entrances or exits from the room.

Koreth growled at him. *To survive the challenge, you must control Lycos.*

"And if I can't?"

"You die." A violet cloud shimmered in the room, and the same woman he remembered from his last visit stepped into view, the clouds dissipating after her arrival.

Nate stood and briefly bowed to her. "First Mother."

"Greetings, Son of my Son's Son." Her sad smile tugged at Nate. "You attempted to remove the medallions, even though you were told you would die should they be taken from you."

"I did."

"Why?"

"Lycos tried to kill my mate. I could not permit that."

Her dark hair fluttered, though Nate didn't feel a breeze. He felt her touch his mind, then she smiled. "You would die to protect her."

"I would give my life for her. For anyone in my pack."

Her smile was radiant. "I knew we were right to trust you." Her hand touched his face.

The walls of the room faded into nothing, replaced by more clouds. Nate turned, his gaze sweeping the area. "Where am I?"

"This is the Arena. Long ago you learned you have the power within you to become two, man and wolf. We kept full knowledge of your abilities from you, not knowing for sure our trust was properly placed." Her smile became sad. "I fear your difficulties stem from ignorance of your full power. Without knowledge, you have no way to master your Lycos, the embodiment of the power within your bloodline." Her gaze searched his eyes. "Lycos is not another, as Koreth is. Lycos is you. The personification of your power. You must be in control of yourself to survive."

She curled her left-hand and swept it right to left in front of her body. Violet light streamed from her hand, swirled and tightened around him.

Fear struck him. "Wait, I can't go back. I can't protect my mate from Lycos!"

The First Mother's gentle voice caressed him. "You will return to your world when you have control of the beast within. Without control, you will never return to Earth."

Violet clouds dissolved, taking the First Mother with them. Her voice whispered in his mind. *You are Lycos. Lycos is you. Control yourself.*

Nate whirled when a snort sounded behind him. Lycos stood in the clouds, startled eyes looking at Nate. "What have you done, Human?"

Chapter 16

Things were going much better than Jonathan expected after Nate's abrupt disappearance. It didn't hurt anything that Eli showed up. After seeing Nate's power, the other Alphas seemed unwilling to test their strength against Eli. Jonathan turned one of the steaks he was grilling, then one-by-one turned the rest.

Their guests were seated in the picnic shelter, talking quietly, and being waited on by the teens. He snickered, remembering the fuss when the boys were ordered to help the girls wait on the tables. Nate systematically destroyed all the male or female stereotypes he could. If someone preferred to cook and clean, or fix motors and mow the lawn, he didn't prevent it. He just refused to assign tasks according to gender norms. Boys eat, so they need to learn to cook. Girls drive, so they need to learn car maintenance.

The girls seemed to like it a lot more than the guys did. Still, when assigned to wash dishes or some other task that kept them near one or more of the girls, the boys gave only token resistance. Some of the girls, especially Isabella and Paisley, preferred working on ranch vehicles rather than in the house.

Jonathan glanced at Janelle. The edge of white bandages showed at her collar. Her Lupine healing would soon remove the need for them. Renate on one side, Flora on the other, Janelle sat at the head of the largest table. Eli sat on Renate's left. The other Alphas sat at the same table. Retainers brought by their alphas sat at other tables, though they kept their eyes moving, watching for any threat. Captain Fischer's Council Guard stood at attention on the three open sides of the shelter providing extra security.

Murmurs silenced. An eerie hush filled the shelter. Jonathan shut the lid on the grill then turned to see what quieted the group. General Brighton followed Major Rollins to a table. Peyton and his two kids, as well as a man needing a shave and wearing a Huntsmen uniform, sat at the same table. With a sigh, Jonathan walked over to them. Too aware of the silence surrounding him, he nodded to the general. "Afternoon, General. Want some steak?"

"Sounds good, Dyers. Just wave it over the grill and bring it on."

Jonathan shivered. "Why not just eat it raw?"

"Bothers the people I'm eating with."

With a laugh, Jonathan nodded. "One barely flame-kissed steak coming up." He glanced at Peyton, Paige, Phillip, and the Huntsman. "And the rest of you?"

Peyton grinned. "Medium-well for me." Paige and Phillip nodded. The Huntsman with them was too busy looking around to notice the question.

Paige tapped his hand. "Want your steak medium-well, Lee?"

Lee jerked his gaze to Paige, then looked up at Jonathan with a nod. "Medium-well is fine."

"One very rare and four medium-well. One of the kids will bring it over when it's done." Jonathan's eyes flicked to Paige, then back to the Huntsman. "After lunch, get him something different to wear."

Paige grimaced and glanced at Lee. "I'll take care of it. Lee, this is Jonathan Dyers. He's Nate's Beta, um, second-in-command. Jonathan, Lee Hill."

The young man swallowed and glanced up at Jonathan. "Good to meet you, Sir."

Jonathan raised an eyebrow at Peyton. "He a prisoner?"

Peyton rocked his hand in the air. "Yes and no. He just met a friendly vampire for the first time. Claims he wants to help. We'll see."

At the large table, someone cleared his throat. Jonathan turned and found Prince Hansh standing behind him. "Excuse me," the prince said. "You said he met a vampire?"

When Jonathan glanced over his shoulder, the general met his gaze and sighed. Without turning to face the prince, Brighton said. "I am a vampire."

How can silence get any quieter? Jonathan rolled his eyes and turned to face Hansh. "General Brighton has been fighting against V-Triumph his entire life."

The prince gave Jonathan a dismissive glance, then studied Brighton's back. "If you're a vampire, too, why fight V-Triumph? Why not join them?"

Brighton turned on his bench to face the prince but didn't stand. Jonathan swallowed his relief. Had Brighton jumped to his feet, one of the Alphas' guards might have decided he was a threat. Leaning toward the prince, the general sighed. "Feeding on humans and *were* is forbidden by the Progenitors. Those aligned with V-Triumph choose to defy the Progenitors' Laws. I and others like me are Covenant Vampires. We strive to stop the human slaughter by defeating those evil enough to feed on sentient beings."

His gaze flicked past the prince to each of the Alphas and Queens. He winked at Janelle. "I am no threat to any of you." With that, he turned back to the table and looked up at Jonathan. "Think we might have some of that salad?"

Biting his tongue to prevent his laugh, Jonathan nodded. In all the times the general visited the ranch, if he ate anything, it was never a salad. Brighton once said salad was food his food ate. Without commenting on Brighton's statement, he motioned for Reese to bring salads to the general's table.

Jonathan went back to his grill but watched from the corner of his eye to see if Brighton ate the salad Reese brought him. He hid his grin behind his hand when Brighton shivered just before opening his mouth and taking a huge bite of lettuce and tomatoes. Jonathan smothered his snort. *Who said vampires aren't funny?*

"Flora!" Numerous gasps followed Will's shout.

Meat fork in hand, Jonathan whirled to see what upset Will, Flora's Tom. The panther shifter was standing looking around, expression frantic. Startled cries jerked Jonathan's attention to the visitors in the picnic shelter. One-by-one, each Alpha or Queen shimmered, then disappeared, leaving only Prince Hansh. Dropping the meat fork, Jonathan ran toward Janelle. Before he could get to her, Snarl jumped to stand beside her. Just as Snarl's hand rested on her shoulder, Janelle disappeared, then Eli and Daryll. Last, General Brighton vanished.

Benches overturned and crashed to the concrete floor.

Snarls and growls filled the air as retainers and guards turned to face those who must have taken their Alphas and Queens. Being the only leader left behind, their anger turned toward Prince Hansh. Iridescent mist showered over them, left them all frozen. A disembodied voice sounded, speaking in a strange tongue that all somehow understood.

"The First Mother calls those who rule her people to witness the trial of the Royal *Were* King. You will not harm each other. So, says the First Mother."

Chapter 17

Staggering, Nate took a step back, then leaned over, hands on his knees. A shimmer of violet light brought his head up. When the light faded, the leaders Lycos summoned to the ranch stood high above him. The clouds obscured whatever they were standing on, but it reminded Nate of an arena with bleachers above the walls. More appeared, including Janelle, Eli, Daryll, and then General Brighton. Others unknown to him appeared. Nate turned to look at the people surrounding him. Shouts and questions filled the air. Somehow, he knew all the Alphas he called to the ranch were present, as well as those he had not yet called. Every Alpha from every *were* group on Earth.

"Nate!" Eli shoved to the front of the crowd, leaned over the edge of whatever he was standing on, and looked down at him, Janelle and Brighton at his shoulders. "What's happening?"

"There will be silence!" Following the echoing voice, a brighter violet glow shimmered beside Nate, and the First Mother appeared. "This, the Son of my Son's Son, is challenged to control the powers of his bloodline." She turned in a slow circle to meet the gaze of each Alpha or Queen. "Should he succeed, I shall crown him Royal *Were* King, King of All *Were*. Should he fail, he will die. You will witness the challenge in silence."

Abrupt silence was almost palpable. She turned to Nate. The First Mother raised her arm, her finger pointing at him. Violet light showered him. "You are given full knowledge of your heritage and your power."

Nate staggered as the weight of his abilities filled his mind.

"Should you fail, you will die."

Janelle's gasp snagged his attention.

"Should you die..." The First Mother waited until Nate looked at her. "Should you die, all these will die here, as well."

"What? No! You can't..."

The First Mother waved her hand at him. Nate's voice caught in his throat, and he was unable to speak. His left hand clasped his throat.

"Only one with the full power of the bloodline has the power to leave this place unassisted. I am forbidden to assist. For them to return to your world, the Royal King, you, must return them home." A sad smile touched her lips but didn't make it to her eyes. "If you fail, the Royal line will continue through your daughter. Eventually, another will be born to take your place. If your world survives long enough."

Her expression softened. "You, Grandson, are the Royal Lycos and King. For the time of the challenge, your powers are confined to the Arena. Accept yourself that you all may live!" She was gone. No shimmer. No glimmer. No glow. Just. Gone.

Nate swallowed and lifted his gaze to Janelle. For a moment, she looked terrified, then she relaxed. Her gentle smile warmed him. "You can do this. You are our champion, Nate. Conquer Lycos and take us home."

He let his gaze move around the audience the Mother brought and swallowed. *I can't let them die!*

Chapter 18

Arms crossed over his chest, Nate turned to face Lycos. Head tilted, he studied the wolfman while absently noting his throat was no longer frozen quiet. Lycos stood four feet taller than Nate, saliva dripping from his teeth. The wolfman threw his head back, his roar echoing through the clouds. Lycos mumbled something then swirled his hands through the air, catching particles of light. He gathered the light into a large glowing ball, then threw it at Nate.

Nate dove to the right. The edge of the glowing ball brushed the hem of his jeans and left the fabric smoldering. Ignoring the heat on his ankle, Nate rolled to his feet and dropped into a defensive stance. *How can I fight Lycos if Lycos is me?*

Koreth's voice whispered in his mind. *Acceptance and control is the key.*

Acceptance? Control? Of what? Nate dodged another burning ball of light Lycos slammed at him. Lycos' roar echoed. Before the echo died, Lycos charged. Nate braced for the attack, then blinked when Lycos ran past him. He whipped around. Lycos ran toward Janelle. *No!* "No!"

Pulling from the knowledge forced into his mind, Nate pulled long streams of brilliant light together, forming them into a spear. With a quick step, he hurled the light weapon toward Lycos' back. The light-spear struck Lycos between the shoulders and forced him to his knees. After a dazzling pulse, the spear dissolved.

Nate tackled Lycos. Rolling with him, Nate pushed the

wounded wolfman to his back and straddled his chest. Nate's knees pressed into Lycos' shoulders, trapping his arms. "I won't let you hurt Janelle!"

Lycos roared and shoved at Nate. "She makes us weak."

"She makes me strong! Without her, I have nothing." Nate wrapped his hands around the wolfman's throat. Beneath Nate's hands, light laced around Lycos' throat, then slowly tightened. Nate blinked, startled to hear a growl from deep in his own throat. "You will not hurt her! I'll kill you first!" Lycos struggled, but couldn't get Nate's hands and the magic between them off his neck.

Accept that you may be whole. Koreth's voice filtered through Nate's fury. The memory of the First Mother's words came back to him. *Control that you all may live!*

Nate took a deep breath, swallowed his anger and looked at Lycos. Really looked at him. With a wave of his hand, the light strangling Lycos faded to nothing. Nate rolled off Lycos' chest and sat on his heels facing him. Lycos lunged to his knees, then stopped and stared at Nate. Waiting.

"I could kill you without half trying."

Lycos didn't move.

"But you can't hurt me. Not mortally, anyway."

Lycos raised an eyebrow but didn't speak.

"If I can kill you, why can't you hurt me?" Puzzled, Nate looked past Lycos to Janelle. He ignored the eyes of the Alphas. He wouldn't let anything happen to them, but their approval wasn't important. Janelle bit her lip, fear in her eyes. Then he realized her fear wasn't for her, it was for him. His eyes stung with the realization and he swallowed.

Turning his gaze back to Lycos, he tilted his head and studied him. *Fractured.* Koreth's thought slipped into his mind. Nate considered the word, then searched his memory to find the break.

*****

"Incoming!" Hands on the controls, Nate twisted the helicopter to the side, trying to avoid the missile on his screen. Behind him, men shouted as the sharp move caused them to tumble around the interior. Sharp relief filled his chest when the missile whistled by just inches from the fuselage. Relief short-lived. Another missile sped from the surface. The explosion rocked the chopper, ripping the fuselage open. Searing heat engulfed Nate.

A fireball in the sky, the chopper spun to the ground, crashing in the burning Afghanistan sand. The jar brought him to his senses. Heat everywhere. His team burning, screams filling his ears, then gone. Only the roar of flames. Fumbling with hands burned beyond functioning, he finally got his harness open and stumbled into the cabin. Only Kelly was alive. Catching him beneath the arms, Nate yanked him over his shoulder, clutched a rifle, jumped from the open door, and stumbled toward the ruins of an old building.

Staggering the last few steps, he dropped to his knees, charred fabric doing nothing to protect his flesh from gritty sand. Gently, he settled Kelly in the meager shade. He sat up to peer over blocks of stone. Even from here, the chopper's burning heat hit him. *I couldn't save them!*

Anguish for his lost team ripped through him. His last mission before re-enlistment and he failed them! Kelly moaned. Nate unbuckled his helmet and gently removed it. The helmet protected most of Kelly's red curls from flames. Short as it was, his hair refused to follow regulations. Nate sobbed. Kelly was terribly burned. Nate didn't dare to try to remove the jacket, afraid the charred mess was seared into his skin. He needed a hospital.

Keying the radio on his belt, Nate frowned. No signal. Damaged in the crash, no doubt. Kelly's moan morphed into a scream. Nate wanted to hold his hand, but Kelly's hands were burned even more than his own. "Kelly," he whispered.

Kelly caught his breath and opened his eyes. Anguish extinguished the sparkle he usually saw there. "What happened?"

"Missile. I couldn't shake the second one." His bitter self-recrimination sounded harsh in his ears.

Blinking, Kelly focused on Nate's face. "The team?"

"All gone. We're all that's left."

Kelly closed his eyes for a moment, then looked at him and gave him a slight head shake. "You're all that's left, Colonel. You have to get the intel back to Brighton."

"They'll send someone for us."

"No. They won't. Off the books, remember?" He shuddered and strangled on a low moan. "You have to go, Nate."

"I won't leave you here."

"You don't have a choice." He coughed. "I'm not going to make it."

"No! You..."

"Stop, Lieutenant Colonel!" Kelly's gaze searched Nate's face. "Nate, I'm dying. I have internal injuries that won't heal. I won't survive." Pink foam frothed at his lips.

"But..."

"Listen to me!"

"I'm listening."

"Brighton doesn't know. Don't tell him."

"Tell him what?"

"Don't tell him you were burned."

"I...I don't understand."

"Look at your hands, Nate."

Nate held his hands up. The seared flesh was gone, replaced by new, pink skin. He shook his head. "I don't understand."

"You're special, Nate. Don't ever forget that. You're special!" Colonel Kelly Taren smiled, then flinched. "Get that intel to headquarters." With a gasp, he moaned. Breath rattled in his chest for the last time.

*****

Clouds swirled around Nate. He blinked and looked at his hands. He remembered Kelly dying. Remembered staggering through miles of sand and heat, avoiding unfriendlies. Remembered giving the intel to Brighton, but until this minute, he'd forgotten his hands healed even before Kelly died. He blamed himself for their deaths and resigned his commission when his enlistment was served.

He deserved his wounds for letting his team die, but even before he walked out of the desert and into the ground base, his wounds completely healed. The physical wounds, but not the emotional ones. Healing he did not deserve. "I've been broken since the helicopter crash."

Koreth agreed. *Fractured. Yes.*

How did Kelly know? What did he know? Nate sensed Koreth's uncertainty. He raised his eyes to Lycos. *Lycos is part of me.* Again, he felt Koreth agree. *To be in control, I must accept all of me. All of us. The good, the bad, the damaged.*

Nate stood up. "I won't destroy myself. My life is committed to the First Mother's charge, my mate, and my daughter. I am *Were* King."

Lycos stood, too. While Nate watched, Lycos's expression calmed. Nate extended his hand to Lycos to shake the wolfman's clawed hand. Lycos dropped his gaze to Nate's hand, then tilted his head and reached forward. As their hands touched, Lycos dissipated into the air and settled into Nate's mind next to Koreth. For the first time, he could access Lycos as easily as he could the wolf. *Whole!*

Moist clouds brushed against his back. He turned and found the First Mother standing in the Arena. In her hands, she held a silver circlet. "Kneel, Son of my Son's Son."

Nate blinked, then dropped to his knees.

"You have accepted your full potential. From this point, you have full control of your abilities and your heritage." She set the silver band on his head.

The silver band flared, sinking through his hair. Tickles swirled across his scalp as the band melded into his flesh, becoming a part of him. From the Alpha's he heard a low murmur. Silver burned most *were*. Those it didn't burn broke out in a severe rash, and constant contact scarred. He could sense the heat in the metal, but his flesh didn't burn.

"You will wear the True King's crown until your last breath, but only *were* and vampires will have a clear sight of it." First Mother stepped back, then gave him a shallow curtsy. "All hail the Royal Alpha *Were* King!" She vanished.

Nate stood and faced the Alphas and Queens. Slowly, first a few, then as one, they dropped to one knee and bowed their heads. "All hail the Royal Alpha *Were* King!"

Chapter 19

While the Alphas knelt, the stands they were in sank lower in the clouds until they were on the same level as Nate. Gazing at heads bowed to him, Nate swallowed. There were hundreds of Alphas of all kinds of shifters, as well as General Brighton. *Brighton must be the commander of all the Covenant Vampires the First Mother mentioned.* Nate gave him a single nod, then raised an eyebrow when he saw Daryll, Flora, and Eli kneeling around Janelle.

Again, Nate was given authority he never asked for. But this time, he took a deep breath, squared his shoulders, and accepted the responsibilities of the Royal Alpha *Were* King. "Rise."

All stood, waiting for him to speak.

"In our world, V-Triumph vampires are threatening to destroy the *were* so they may enslave humans. It is the duty of *were* to safeguard humans, even though they may not deserve it at times. V-Triumph has created a human army, the Huntsmen, to aid in our destruction."

He slowly turned on his heel, his gaze touching each in the crowd. "Does any deny the First Mother crowned me?"

No one spoke. "Then the coronation is done." Nate waited to see if anyone would speak.

When none did, he took a deep breath and continued. "The Huntsmen are duped into believing they are the saviors of humankind, saving them from us. Unless there is no other way, the Huntsmen will not be killed, but will instead be captured and retrained. We've discovered that most will join us when they learn the truth. Those who will not join us will have their memories erased and be left to live their lives as they wish."

I can't tell how they're taking all this, he silently said to Koreth. Koreth answered, *They're stunned, but none object.* Nate sent a silent thank you to Koreth, then gave his full attention back to the gathered leaders. "Before returning you each to your homes, I am taking you to Texas to the ranch. There we will meet and discuss how to proceed. Objections?" There were none.

"So be it." Nate swept his left arm in a circle, brought his right hand up to meet the left, then hands forming c-shapes, he pulled them apart. A deep blue smoke billowed from his hands, rushing outward and covering all the Alphas. A slight shiver zinged down his spine, then the blue smoke wisped away. The Alphas startled when they realized they were standing on grass instead of clouds. "This is the Challenge Field. Do any wish to challenge for the crown?"

No one spoke. *Quiet bunch.* Inwardly grinning at Koreth's assessment, Nate walked to Janelle. He took her hand and pulled her to the center. "This is Janelle Rollins, my mate, my wife, and my *Were* Queen of Royal blood."

The assembled Alphas bowed deeply to Janelle, then stood. Unable to repress the grin longer, Nate turned to Janelle. "I don't know about everyone else, but I'm starved."

She laughed. *You're always hungry,* he heard in his mind. Aloud, she said, "When we left, Jonathan was grilling steaks. Let's see if there are any left." Taking his hand, his mate pulled him through the parting crowd. They followed their King and Queen out of the Challenge Field, across the compound, around the house, to the picnic shelter. Benches overturned as *were* rushed to their Alphas.

Jonathan raised an eyebrow. "The First Mother said you were on trial."

Nate's grin turned sheepish. He fisted Jonathan's shoulder. "I had to overcome her challenge to be crowned King."

Jonathan's gaze rested on the silver band on Nate's forehead. "I knew you'd be back." He glanced past Nate at the crowd behind him, then shrugged and refocused on his Alpha. "I think we're going to have to buy some more steaks."

Janelle laughed, and Nate smiled into her upturned face. She motioned toward the warehouse. "We have a hundred pounds of chicken breasts in the walk-in. And about as much sausage. Let's grill that."

Three hours later, Nate called the first Royal Council to order. Since they didn't have enough chairs or benches for everyone, the Council was convened in the Challenge Field. Nate stood on an old wood pallet, Snarl and Jonathan behind him, while the world's Alphas sat on tarps spread on the grass. After hours of discussion and argument, the Council decided the Alpha of each pack, clowder, pride, den, leap, murder or other designation of *were* group would select one representative to make up the King's World Enclave.

When the meeting ended, Nate wisped the Alpha's who had not been already at the ranch to their homes. *It would be interesting to be a fly on the wall when they reappeared as suddenly as they disappeared.* He grinned at Koreth's thought. Those on the ranch would have to return by plane to avoid government investigation. When the blue mist subsided, Nate bit his lip and looked out over the ranch. *The inn will work temporarily, but we'll need housing for the reps.*

He gazed past the new house close to the fish pond. Beyond the pond, there was plenty of room for something. Frowning in thought, head cocked to the left, he ignored the activity around him as Alpha's who were staying at the inn prepared to leave. An apartment building would work. Or an inn-type building. With five-hundred bedrooms, it would comfortably house the reps. Meals could be served in a cafeteria setting. He shook his head. *This is getting more complicated all the time. We'll need someone to work the cafeteria once it's built. Could we get permits to build that? Do we even need permits?* He sighed and went to find Jonathan and General Brighton.

Chapter 20

Lee stood at a window in the ranch office. When the Alphas disappeared from the picnic shelter, Jonathan asked Major Rollins to move the humans to the office where they could be protected if the *were* guests caused problems. Still struggling to accept more shifters than just wolves existed, Lee worried his bottom lip between his teeth.

He turned his back to the window and studied the people sitting around a large oval conference table. Maria and Gisele Schneider, Zoe's mother and aunt respectively, Phillip and Paige Marston, and Lieutenant Donald Dunn. *And me. That makes six humans here.* All the humans except Lt. Dunn were former Huntsmen. Lee clenched his jaw, pulled out a rolling desk chair and sat down.

Lips pursed, brows low over his eyes, he glanced at each of the humans. "So. How come they didn't change us?"

Paige let out a snort of disgust. "I already told you. They won't do that without good cause. They don't force anyone to be *were*."

"Your dad and Zoe both are."

When Paige jumped to her feet, Phillip pulled her back into her chair and sighed. Ignoring his sister, he frowned at Lee. "Dad and Zoe were dying. Dad chose it. Zoe was injured and unconscious, but after the fact, she absolved Daryll of any wrongdoing." His hand still on Paige's arm, Phillip leaned toward Lee. "Knowing what you know

now, would you prefer to die?"

Lee met the glare in Phillip's eyes for a moment, then let out a long breath. "No. I don't think so. I don't know." He ducked his head, then shrugged. "Maybe."

Lieutenant Dunn yawned and stretched. "It's a moot point, anyway. Nothing can be done to reverse it, and they don't seem to be unhappy about it. It's just another form of prejudice. Either you can accept that *were* exist and are not out to eat you or you don't. Just like any group of individuals, there are some bad apples, but most are decent people."

"How long have you known about them?"

Dunn met his stare. "Several months, now. It was a shock to me, too, but they're not bad people. At least not the *were* here." He lifted one shoulder. "Don't know about the rest. Haven't met them."

"So, why are we locked in the office?"

Paige rolled her eyes. "We're not locked in. Lee, we are more easily damaged than the *were* are. Nate promised to keep us safe."

Lee huffed, then glanced at Gisele. Her hands were folded together on the tabletop. He stared at her hands for a moment, then looked at her face. A quick glance confirmed Paige's and Phillip's were missing, too. "What happened to your ring?"

Gisele's voice was quiet, reserved. "The Alpha had it removed."

Lee considered that statement. "But how? The poison..."

Paige leaned back in her chair and crossed her arms over her chest. "Daryll figured out a way to remove them without killing us. We'll remove your ring, too, once all this is over."

"Why?"

"It's a tracker, Lee. While you wear it, they know you are alive and where you are. You were sent here, so they already know you're here. Once it's removed, the Triumvirate will think you're dead. The tracker stops when the ring comes off or your heart stops beating."

"A tracker." Lee tilted his head and frowned at Paige. "Are you that paranoid?"

"No. And I'm not so stubborn not to believe it when someone tells me the truth, either."

Gisele's soft voice cut off Lee's response. "She's telling the truth, Lee."

He studied the resignation on Gisele's face, then turned to look at Paige. "Why would they have trackers on us?"

"Farmers and ranchers sometimes tag their animals." Paige's voice was flat, monotone. "The Triumvirate doesn't want to lose their human cattle, either."

Lee's former training tried to reassert, made him want to deny what he was told. But, for the first time, the full understanding of a human's worth to the Triumvirate crashed into his mind. Terror shivered down his spine. Lee gasped and fell back in his chair. "Cattle. They look at us like cattle?"

The expressions on the faces of those around the table made it real. Closing his eyes, Lee dropped his chin against his collar and took deep even breaths, trying to push back the tunnel vision that was closing in on him. He thought again about the faint scars on his neck and on

Paige's. *We're nothing but food to them.*

Chapter 21

Nate spoke to each remaining Alpha before he or she boarded the SUV to return them to the inn for the night. Tomorrow, they would all be making plans to return to their homes. When they selected their representatives, Nate offered to bring them to the ranch using Lycos' powers to keep them off the government's radar.

After Nate assured them the SUVs would be available to take them to the San Antonio International Airport, they left in the SUVs assigned to them. Nate turned to find Prince Hansh behind him.

"Your Highness, I need to speak with you."

Nate crossed his arms over his chest. "You want to know why you were left here when the others were taken."

"My father was here earlier. He told me the First Mother took him, instead."

With a shrug, Nate motioned for Hansh to follow him to the picnic shelter. After they both sat at one of the tables, Nate put both elbows on the table and leaned forward. "How is your father? I didn't have much time to talk with him."

"He was too ill to make the trip here, so I came in his stead. He seems better now, though."

"He looked well." Nate relaxed and rolled his shoulders. Today's tension was off the charts, and he was tired. "I think something in the air of the Progenitor's homeworld helps with healing."

"Father accepted you as *Were* King. I have been tasked

to stay here as the representative of my Pride."

Nate's left thumb drummed on the picnic table. "I thought you'd be staying, instead of returning home."

Hansh's eyes focused on Nate's forehead. Studying the crown bestowed by the First Mother, no doubt. He blinked, then met Nate's gaze, and nodded. "It is his wish."

"Without objection?" A feral grin traced Nate's lips.

Hansh lowered his head in an informal bow, then again met Nate's gaze. "Without objection."

Nate's grin became friendly. "In that case, have you ever lived in an RV? Until we can get more housing built, we're short on quarters. Otherwise, you'll have to stay at the inn and travel back and forth."

"I have never stayed in an RV. I look forward to it."

"How many people do you have with you?"

"Four."

"If you don't mind sharing quarters, the RV will house up to eight." Nate tilted his head and waited for Hansh's answer.

"I shall consider it an adventure."

"Good." Nate called Jonathan over. "Hansh and his men will be moving to the ranch tomorrow. Have one of the empty RVs prepared for them."

"No problem. I'll have Adrian and Bobby get one ready." Jonathan started to turn away, then jerked back. "Was there anything else, Your Highness?"

Nate huffed. "Don't start that. I thought we already got past that stuff."

"When you were Alpha, but not King."

"You are my number one advisor, then and now. I

expect you to continue behaving the same as always."

A slight smile touched Jonathan's lips. "Understood. Oh, I had the humans taken to your office while the Alphas were missing. I figured it would be the easiest place to protect them since the house was already set up to protect the kids." He shrugged. "There was quite an uproar for a while."

"Good thinking." Nate turned back to Hansh. "We'll have your RV ready for you to move into tomorrow. Until tomorrow, then." He stood and put his hand toward Hansh.

Hansh hesitated, shook Nate's hand, then bowed. "Until tomorrow, Your Highness." He turned and walked to his group.

Nate sighed and glanced at Jonathan. "Is there any way to keep them from calling me that?"

Jonathan laughed. "Maybe. You can try."

Shaking his head and heaving a deep sigh, Nate walked toward the house. Along the way, General Brighton and Janelle stepped out of the dark. Janelle took his hand in hers. In the house, they sent the children to their own homes, then walked upstairs together.

Nate stopped at the office door. "Peyton's kids, Zoe's family, and Lee Hill are inside. I have to take care of this before I join you."

Janelle raised up on her toes and pressed a kiss to his lips. "I'll be waiting." With a come-hither smile, she walked to their bedroom.

For a moment, he considered following her and letting someone else deal with the people in his office. He watched her until the door shut between them and sighed.

Sometimes duty was onerous. Shaking himself, he opened the office door and stepped inside before he could change his mind.

Chapter 22

The six humans on the ranch were confined to the office. *Well, not confined so much as asked to stay here*, Don reminded himself. *For our own safety*. Totally bored, he watched Lee draw circles on the back of Paige's hand using his forefinger. He glanced at Phillip's pressed lips and narrowed eyes. For whatever reason, Phillip wasn't happy with Lee. Paige caught Phillip's glare and jerked her hand away from Lee. Don leaned his elbow on the conference table and rested his chin in his hand, his forefinger covering his mouth. Laughing probably wouldn't go over very well.

The door opened and Nate stepped into the office. General Brighton followed him in, then shut the door behind them. Don sat up straight and watched Nate glance at each of the six humans, before sitting in his executive's chair. General Brighton sat beside him. Before the Alpha spoke, someone knocked on the door, then Daryll stuck his head inside. "Nate, Zoe and I are headed home. Are Marie and Gisele free to join us?"

Nate nodded. "Sure. You can fill them in on what's happened."

With murmured good nights, the two women left with Daryll. Don was amused to see Lee's gaze follow them out. The door closed and Don turned his attention to Nate and the other three humans still in the office.

"For the time being, Don, assign one of the bunks in the Marine Shack to Lee."

"He can bunk in my room for now."

Don left unspoken the offer to keep an eye on the Huntsman but knew Nate understood it, even so.

"Sounds good." Nate turned to study Lee. "So, Huntsman, what have you decided?"

"Decided? About what?" Lee's tone was even, but his rigid posture indicated his distress.

"You can join us and stay here. You can leave after we remove your memory of the ranch, or you can join General Brighton's Elite Forces." Nate put his elbows on the table and steepled his hands. "Regardless of your choice, the ring comes off."

Lee looked down at the ring and bit his lip. "And if I want to go back to HQ?"

"Sorry. Not a choice I can allow." Nate glanced at Paige. "You said Paige is your girlfriend."

"She is."

At the same time, Paige said, "I'm not."

Nate's lips quirked. "Well, which is it?"

Lee and Paige looked at each other. For several long seconds, neither spoke, then Paige sighed and turned to Nate. "It's a long story, Nate. We dated for a couple of years, then he cheated on me."

"I didn't!"

Seeming to forget they had an audience, the two started arguing. Nate slapped the table. Lee and Paige both jumped in their chairs, their attention abruptly jerked to Nate. "That's enough. Paige, why do you think he cheated on you?"

"I saw him at the movies, hugging Stacy Ann." She glared at Lee.

Don smothered a snicker at the long-suffering on

Nate's face. Nate turned to Lee. "Okay, Lee. Do you deny being with Stacy Ann?"

Lee glanced at the glare on Paige's face. Nate cleared his throat. "Don't look at Paige. Look at me."

Lee turned his gaze to Nate. "No. I was with her, but we were not on a date." He looked at Paige. "I tried to tell you..."

"Look at me, Huntsman! Tell me what happened."

Lee's gaze lurched back to Nate. "Stacy Ann and Mark were at the movies. They had a fight, and he left her there. She called the base for a ride home. I was the only one there not on duty, so I went to get her. She was crying so hard she couldn't see where she was going. I put my arm around her to help her. She started to fall, and I caught her." Don chuckled when Lee turned again to Paige. "I was not hugging her!"

Paige looked uncertain. "Why was she crying?"

"She...I promised I wouldn't tell, Paige."

"She's dead, Lee. Tell me."

Don glanced at Nate. He seemed comfortable letting the two talk it out at this point. Lee bowed his head. He was quiet. Don counted to ten before Lee spoke again without raising his head. "You're sure she's dead? That vampires fed on her?"

Paige softened her tone. "I'm sure, Lee."

Lee swallowed hard. "She was pregnant with Mark's baby. She wanted to leave the Huntsmen. Mark refused to go. Until later."

"Did you report them?"

At Paige's quiet question, Lee shook his head. "They were friends. I couldn't. I don't know how they were

110

found out. You tell me the Triumvirate killed him and fed on her. I just don't know what to make of it."

General Brighton let out a whistle. "That's why they fed on her, instead of just killing her."

Everyone at the table fixed their gaze on the general. He looked at Nate. "The blood of a pregnant female is...sweet...almost intoxicating. Regardless of the species." Brighton took a deep breath. "Even had they not been hungry, the V-Triumph vampires would have fed on her."

"That's real?" Lee's face paled. "They would really do that to her?"

"They would. I have no doubt they did." Brighton's words were firm.

Don blinked at the horror in Lee's eyes. The Huntsman stood and faced Nate. "Sir, I respectfully request you allow me to stay here." His gaze twitched toward Paige, but he controlled the impulse and kept his eyes on the Alpha. "I will do anything to keep that from happening to anyone else."

"You will pledge loyalty to me? To the pack?"

Lee blinked several times but managed to nod. "I will, Sir."

Nate looked at Paige. "Paige?"

Chin trembling and eyes filling with unshed tears, she nodded. "Please, Nate. Keep him here. Keep him safe."

"I can take him into the pack, Paige." His voice gentled. "But I cannot promise to keep him safe. I can't promise any of us are safe until this is over."

"I understand, Sir."

Nate's gaze turned to Lee. "You are willing to

renounce your oath to the Huntsmen?"

"Sir, yes, Sir."

"Koreth, my wolf, will mind-walk to ensure you are truthful in your oath. If you are found false, your memory will be removed, and you will be banished from the pack. Are you willing?"

Lee's Adam's apple bobbed. He shot a glance at Paige, then looked straight ahead. "Sir, yes, Sir!"

Nate stood and shimmered into a wolf. Koreth padded around the table. His head level with Lee's shoulder, he easily gazed into Lee's eyes. After a moment, Lee's eyes closed, and his chin dropped to his chest. Don glanced at Paige. Her breath caught in her chest as she watched. When Koreth stepped back and shimmered into Nate, she pulled her bottom lip into her mouth. Lee sighed and opened his eyes.

"Koreth believes you." Nate put his hand out, shaking Lee's hand when he clasped it. "Welcome to the pack. For now, you're quartered with Don. We'll find you a place of your own as soon as we can. Tomorrow, meet with Major Rollins. Tell him everything you can about the Huntsman's Headquarters."

Lee blinked, nodded, then turned and gave Paige a soft smile. She sniffed, blinking back tears. Nate glanced at her, then grinned. "Looks like you two need some time to talk." He waved at the door. "Go on. Wait at the picnic shelter for Don."

After the two left, Nate sat down. "Don, put him in the same training unit with Phillip. Get him out of that uniform and have Daryll remove his ring." Nate turned to Phillip. "Question?"

"Yes, Sir." Phillip fidgeted. "You, I mean, Koreth corroborated Lee's story about Stacy Ann?"

"He did." Nate raised an eyebrow. "That a problem?"

"No." Phillip drew the word out. "It's just...well, Paige liked him, and she was really hurt. I'm not sure how Dad is going to feel about them getting back together."

"Paige is a grown woman. If she decides to be with Lee, it's her choice."

Nibbling on his lip, Phillip glanced at Don. Don gave him a noncommittal look. Sighing, Phillip lifted both shoulders. "I suppose so."

Nate stood and motioned for the two men to get up. "This has been a long day, and I'm bushed. I'll see you both tomorrow."

"Good night, Nate." Don clapped a hand on Phillip's shoulder and pulled him toward the door. Nate followed them out but turned left toward his bedroom while they turned right to take the stairs.

After Don closed the front door behind them, he turned to face Phillip. "I know you're worried about Paige, Phillip, but you need to back off. She won't appreciate you interfering. Especially if she really likes the guy."

"I know, but..."

"But what?"

"She's my sister!"

Don heaved a heavy sigh. "Your big sister. If Nate thought Lee would hurt her, he'd have told him to stay away from her."

"You think so?"

Cuffing Phillip's shoulder, Don grinned. "Of course. Haven't you noticed that he likes to boss people around."

Phillip gave a startled laugh. "I suppose I have."

"Phillip, Nate takes his responsibility to the people in his pack very seriously. He won't let anyone hurt any of them if he can help it. Since he didn't tell Lee to stay away from her, I think we can assume Nate thinks it'll work out okay." Don grinned at Phillip's concerned face. "Give it a rest. Let's go get them and get some sleep."

Phillip huffed but said nothing. He followed Don to the picnic shelter. Paige and Lee were holding hands and talking in quiet tones. Phillip spoke before Don could. "Time for bed, kids! We have a big day tomorrow."

Chapter 23

Three weeks later, Nate stood at the office window sipping coffee while he watched eight buses and two SUVs pull into the ranch yard. Thankfully, the oil wells were still pumping. Buying eight commercial buses wasn't cheap.

According to Jonathan and Daryll, it would take months to get the housing built, if all the required permits could be acquired. Instead, Nate had Jonathan build a prefab warehouse on the other side of the house Daryll's carpenters built for Netty and her family. The inside was finished out to make a 550-seat amphitheater.

With strict instructions to behave around the human employees, the representatives Lycos brought to Texas were housed at the Texas Bay Inn. Ben, Dottie and her two daughters moved to the inn to manage the place and keep an eye on the *were*. Adrian, Dottie's oldest child, stayed on the ranch to continue his training with the other teens.

Prince Hansh decided to return to the inn, too, citing concerns that some might think he was gaining unwarranted favor by living on the ranch. A dozen of the Council Guard, now renamed the Royal Guard, were stationed at the inn for security.

Twice a week, on alternating days, half the representatives traveled on the buses to the ranch for meetings with Nate and the World Enclave. Nate planned to have them all come at the same time for a full meeting and a meal at least once a month. Meanwhile, they were getting to know each other and Nate. Today was the first of the full meetings.

Nate watched the representatives walk toward the amphitheater. Sighing, he tossed back the last of his coffee, set the mug on his desk, and left the office. His back twitched against the dread settling between his shoulder blades. Being a king living in south Texas still felt...silly.

Jonathan walked in the front door as Nate stepped off the stairs. "Morning, Nate." He tapped the clipboard in his left hand. "All reps are checked in and waiting for you in the amphitheater."

"How's the general mood?"

"Solemn. The information provided by Lee Hill has them all concerned."

Nate flicked a glance at Jonathan and nodded. "Me, too. That's our topic of discussion today."

"Thought as much. You made any decisions, yet?"

"Let me give you a hypothetical. Say someone is planning to kill you and everyone you care about." Nate waited for Jonathan to look at him. "Suppose you know where they are, and you have the numbers to get to them first. To stop what they're planning. What do you do?"

"You've already decided to take the fight to the Huntsmen, haven't you?"

"I have." He ran splayed fingers through his hair, messing up the efforts of his comb. "Will the reps cooperate?"

"I think so." Jonathan tapped the clipboard against his thigh. "After the material Lee offered, they'd be fools not to."

Blowing his breath out, Nate opened the front door. "I think, so, too."

Jonathan's boots thumped across the porch behind Nate and followed him down the steps. Stopping, Nate whirled. "Do we still have some pastries?

"There are a few cases in the warehouse."

"Ask someone to bring them to the meeting and have all the coffee urns and some Styrofoam cups brought in. This is going to be a long meeting."

"Sure thing. What about hot water and tea bags, too, for those who don't drink coffee?"

"Sounds good. Thanks." Nate continued to the amphitheater while Jonathan detoured to the kitchen to find someone to prepare the refreshments. The amphitheater building looked like another aluminum-walled warehouse from the outside, but when Nate opened the door and stepped inside, it was like walking into a formal government building.

Beyond the foyer, four sets of double-doors evenly spaced across the far wall opened into the amphitheater. White walls and multiple chandeliers brightened the room. Thick grey carpeting covered the floors, with 550 comfortably stuffed theater seats arranged at massive wooden tables curved around a dais at the other end of the narrow walkway. Most of the chairs were occupied by World *Were* Representatives. Seating was assigned by drawing after several *were* fought over who sat closest to the king's dais. Nate didn't have the patience to wait for them to decide on a hierarchy.

Glancing around the room, Nate swallowed a chuckle. Only the United Nations Assembly held a more diverse collection of multinationals. Representatives from all the world's major packs, clowders, prides, or other groups of *were* filled the room. Wolves, bears, panthers, lions, foxes, leopards, tigers, and more attended the meeting.

They hadn't noticed Nate, yet. He took the opportunity to watch them interact. So far, no aggression displayed. With a grunt of approval, he walked to Daryll who was talking with Snarl at the back of the room and tapped him on the shoulder. When Daryll turned, Nate waved toward the dais. "Best get this started."

Daryll nodded, pulled out his phone, swiped the screen, then tapped. A loud gong sounded over the speakers, and everyone quietened, standing and bowing when they noticed Nate. Nate looked askance at Daryll. "Phone controlled?"

Daryll grinned. "Phillip is great with electronics."

The corner of Nate's mouth curled up. "Lead the way, Commander."

Daryll's sigh reminded Nate the bear preferred carpentering to enforcing. After bowing to him, Daryll stood and faced the crowd. His bearish voice thundered through the room. "Announcing His Royal Highness, His Majesty, King Nathaniel."

Again, the crowd bowed. Ignoring Snarl's snicker, Nate glanced at Daryll, and whispered, "Nathaniel?"

Daryll shrugged, but his eyes were dancing with humor. "It is your name," he whispered back.

Nate rolled his eyes. Maybe it was his imagination, but his steady, carpet-muffled footsteps sounded more confident than he felt. Snarl followed him. When he reached the dais, Nate stepped behind the desk in front of the massive oak throne the *were* insisted he use. "Please sit." Snarl stood at parade rest behind Nate's left shoulder.

Clothing rustled as the assembled reps sat. Based on suggestions offered by Snarl to start each meeting by giving an opportunity for the reps to make requests or statements, Nate tapped his knuckle against the top of his desk to open the meeting. "Are there any petitions?"

A tall, slender man stood three rows back from the front. "Your Majesty." He waited until Nate nodded for him to continue. "Queen Ji-ae, of the Daegu Fox Skulk of South Korea sends a petition for a boon from King Nathaniel."

"What is it she wants?" Nate pressed his left-hand flat against his desktop to keep his thumb still. Thrumming it against the tabletop would betray his anxiety. And that, he refused to do.

"Queen Ji-ae submits that it would be advantageous for your daughter to mate outside the wolves. She requests her son be considered as promised mate to Princess Ophelia."

Shouts filled the air as the reps argued which shifter group should have the honor of selecting a mate for the princess. Nate's palm slapped the desktop; the smack crashed through the speakers. The representatives turned startled gazes to Nate. Narrowed eyes focused tightly on the werefox, Nate leaned forward. "No." The werefox swallowed. When he opened his mouth to speak again, Nate stood up. "Silence!" His roar brought instant quiet.

"My daughter will select her mate." He shook his head and glared at them. "She's not even a year old. I will not bind her to anyone. Her mate is her choice. Not mine."

A weretiger stood in the first row. "Your Highness?"

His calm expression and relaxed posture helped Nate regain some semblance of calm. "Yes?"

The weretiger bowed, then stood and said, "Your Highness, since you are opposed to this, none here will presume so much. However, I submit that you might allow the youth of our clans and tribes the opportunity to meet your daughter when she is older, so she will get to know other *were* her age."

"I'll think about it. This discussion is tabled until later. Much later."

With a bow, the two reps sat down. Nate cleared his throat and let out a silent cleansing breath. "Are there more petitions?"

No one spoke.

"Good." Nate sat on his throne. "It's time to plan our assault on Huntsman Headquarters."

Chapter 24

Uncertain why his presence was required in the meeting, Lee kept his mouth shut and his eyes open. Nate stood at the conference table and frowned at the topographical map covering the end of the table. The *were* called the Royal Council and Brighton stood with Nate on the opposite side of the table from Peyton, Zoe, Phillip, Paige, and Lee. Nate glanced at Peyton, who was standing on Lee's left. "How do they get away with such a large, military compound in the center of the country?"

Peyton leaned forward, tracing a large shape that covered several forested mountains and the open plains west of the site. "There is a total of 1,200 acres. About 800 acres, this non-forested area, is basically a normal ranch with a garden where most of their food is grown. Huntsmen alternate working the ranch and training on the base."

Lee nibbled his bottom lip. The strangeness he felt being with the *were* twisted his stomach into knots. He met Peyton's glance, then Paige's dad pointed at a heavily wooded area on the map. "The rest of the acreage contains the base. Except around the edges for cover, the forest here is not as full as it appears. Huntsmen have owned this land for over a hundred years. As technology progressed, so, too, have their security measures. There is a state-of-the-art mesh canopy that covers the entire base, making it impossible for satellites to locate the base."

"The entire base?" Nate shook his head. "That would be fantastically expensive."

"The inventor was a Huntsman. It's more advanced than anything the military has ever seen." Peyton straightened up and rubbed the back of his neck. "The entire base is surrounded by a security fence with razor wire on the top. Unless you can magic us in, there's no way to get inside without alerting the Huntsmen."

Struggling against the embedded commands to destroy the *were*, Lee clenched his fists. Brighton showed him how the vampires, especially the Supreme Commander, forced him to hate *were*, but knowing and overcoming were not quite the same thing. Breathing shallowly, Lee glanced at Paige. She seemed not to have any reservations about helping them.

Brighton cleared his throat. "What about the base? Do we have a map?"

Zoe nodded and slipped a large square of butcher paper out from under the map and settled it on top. Lee frowned. A detailed pencil drawing of the base covered the square of paper. "This is the layout of the base." She pointed to different areas as she spoke. "The barracks, these ten buildings, are all on the east side of the base. This large building on the south side is the gymnasium. On the north side, is the armory." She looked up at Nate. "Much like American military bases, the only armed Huntsmen on base are the MPs. The Supreme Commander won't allow any others to carry weapons unless they are training or leaving on a mission."

Leaning back over the map, she pointed at another large building. "This three-story building houses the classes Huntsmen are required to attend. The basement is seldom used. To the west of the class building is a small infirmary, and to the west of that is the warehouse. North of the class building..." Her fingertip tapped the top portion of the map. "This five-story building is the admin building. The Commanders live on the top floor."

Peyton leaned forward again and pointed to a building west of the admin building. "These are officer quarters, and the building north of the admin offices is the cafeteria."

Nate crossed his arms over his chest and took a deep breath. "So, how many people are we looking at?"

Peyton shrugged. "It depends on how many are in the field at any given moment. Each barracks holds four squads of ten Huntsmen, so a maximum of four-hundred, plus another two-hundred or so trainers, officers, and support personnel." He tapped his thumb on a large complex to the west of the other buildings. "Support personnel live in the apartment complex." He pointed to the last building. "There are usually at least a hundred Huntsmen in training. They live in that building. Of those, some won't make it and will be transferred to admin as clerks, etc. The rest will be sent to other bases to finish training and join squads there." He turned to face Nate. "The Oklahoma Base is one of the few training sites the Huntsmen have. In addition, there are about sixty Huntsmen working the ranch and farm to the east of the base."

Nate pointed at an almost circular clear area on the map, then glanced at Peyton. "What is this?"

"It's an opening in the canopy for the helicopter the Triumvirate use. After descending below the canopy, they fly at a very low altitude to the helipad on the roof of the admin building." Frowning at the question obvious on Nate's face, Peyton sighed. "Other than the Triumvirate's private vehicle, any chopper coming though the canopy will be shot down by heavy mortars placed here, here, and here." Peyton pointed to three different locations surrounding the opening in the canopy. "No questions asked."

Lee couldn't believe Peyton and Zoe gave the wolves so much information. Breathing shallowly, he fixed his gaze on a small spider spinning a web in the far corner. Peripherally, he saw Brighton lean forward to study the map. "Where do they find their recruits?"

Zoe cleared her throat. "Many are born into a Huntsman family, usually on permanent field assignment, but some come from inner city gangs in Chicago, New York, and a few other large cities."

Nate pulled out his chair and sat down. Elbows on the edge of the topographical map under the base map, he steepled his hands and leaned his chin on his thumbs. He moved his fingers away from his mouth and asked, "Why gangs?"

For a moment, Lee hesitated. Then he thought of the Triumvirate feeding off the Huntsmen. His stomach clenched, and for the first time since Peyton brought him to the meeting, he spoke up. "I can answer that." He rolled up the long sleeves of the western shirt Paige found for him and showed the gang symbols tattooed on his arms to them. "Because no one really cares if they disappear. If anyone notices, it's just assumed someone killed them and hid the bodies. Usually, there's no family to cause problems."

Lee bowed his head for a moment, then sighed and looked at Nate. "They offer a home, food, training, and a life you can't get living on the streets."

Nate sucked air through his teeth and frowned at Lee. "How old were you when they 'recruited' you?"

Recruited. Ha! Forced was more like! "Fifteen. Both my brothers were killed in a gang war." He rolled his sleeves back down and shrugged. "The Huntsmen offered to take me and my mother out of the city, away from the gang's violence. For her safety, I accepted." He shook his head and bitterly added, "Not that I would have been permitted to refuse."

Nate studied the young man, then glanced at Peyton. When Peyton nodded, Nate turned back to Lee. "Is your mother still with them?"

Lee swallowed and his expression grew tight. "She died." *I should tell him!* He gave Nate a belligerent stare. "I killed the wolf that attacked her."

Nate's left eyebrow climbed. "After she attacked him?"

Lee shook his head. "She didn't attack. We were shopping. The wolf jumped us in the mall parking lot. She froze. She didn't even have a weapon with her. He just tore her throat out." Lee's lips trembled and his eyes gleamed. His left shoulder raised and lowered. "So, I shot him."

"You weren't there to hunt him?"

"No. I...I think he followed her back from a mission, though. I never saw him before." Lee twitched and avoided Nate's gaze. "After learning the Huntsmen are being used by vampires, I..." Lee swallowed hard. "The

Huntsmen are the only family I have left. I don't want to see them die." Inside, he cringed at the shrillness of his voice.

Peyton put his hand on Lee's shoulder. "We don't want them to die, Lee. We just want to stop the slaughter of *were*. We'll save as many as we can, but if they refuse to surrender...if they don't surrender, and we both know some of them won't, we may not be able to keep them alive."

"What about the children?" Lee's voice still sounded shrill. He swallowed and tried again. "What will you do with the children?"

Nate surged to his feet and leaned toward Lee. His hands slammed the tabletop; his voice became a growl. "What children?"

Peyton grabbed Lee's shoulder and the older man jerked him around to face him. "Since when are there children at headquarters?"

The fury in Peyton's face was like a physical blow. Lee flinched and swallowed. "Since the Supreme Commander ordered squads to kidnap them so he could raise them to be Huntsmen. They're kept in the basement of the class building."

"How many?"

Flicking his gaze at Nate, Lee swallowed again. The glow in Nate's eyes pierced him. It was all he could do not to soil his pants. "Twenty-five, maybe thirty when I left. Maybe more, now."

Chapter 25

In the Oklahoma Huntsman Headquarters, three Triumvirate commanders sat at a table. Low lighting protected their sensitive eyes, allowing them to drop their hoods to their shoulders and remove the sunglasses they wore even when walking the canopy-shaded grounds to the building. Supreme Commander Reyes shoved the weekly reports in front of him to one side. "Has Colonel Lee been in contact?"

Subcommander Vogt leaned back in his chair. "His locator died this morning. He's assumed caught and destroyed."

Reyes frowned but before he spoke, Subcommander Richter shifted and turned to pin the Supreme Commander with a glare. "The Texas pack has cost us numerous operatives, and we still have no information concerning their activities." He lowered his eyebrows at Reyes. "I say it's time to stage a full-scale attack!"

Thunder rumbled. The Supreme Commander stood, walked to the heavily shaded window, and stared at the hills surrounding the complex. He peered through the almost translucent canopy. Translucent from the ground, anyway. *Odd. Not a cloud in the sky.*

In the distance, leaves fell from the trees, swirling like ribbons of orange, red and brown. Most of the forest remained covered in the golden crown of autumn. Here and there were speckled spots of green vegetation. Shifting his gaze closer, he watched uniformed squads of Huntsmen march in formation across the shaded courtyard. The mesh film they had stretched over all the buildings and grounds kept them in perpetual shade but ensured satellites, jets, and planes overhead wouldn't see anything but trees and more trees. He took a deep breath, then sighed. "Without reconnaissance, there's less likelihood of success."

Vogt tapped his foot. Reyes rolled his eyes, annoyed by the nervous tapping. It never failed that when he needed quiet to think, Vogt was tapping that foot.

"So," Vogt said, "recall all missions and take them all to Texas."

Hands clasped behind him while watching the marching soldiers, Reyes contemplated the idea. "If that many Huntsmen converge on a small area in Texas, the local government will get involved." He bowed his head and stared at his feet. "Still, eight squads attacked the ranch, and none returned. Something's definitely going on." A strange feeling settled between his shoulder blades. After a moment, he identified it as the first stirring of fear. "We must find out what that is."

He turned to face his compatriots, but screams jerked him around, his gaze going back to the courtyard. Hundreds of wolves, panthers, lions, leopards, bears, and foxes tore through the grounds, herding unarmed Huntsmen into groups. A siren screeched alarm over the speakers.

Mouth agape, he stumbled and caught himself against the window sash. A crash of thunder pealed, followed by a flash of light and roiling smoke. For a moment, Reyes thought lightning struck the center of the grounds. A huge wolf-man creature stepped out of the smoke.

Reyes took a step back from the window. "It's not possible," he whispered. "Lycos isn't real. He's a children's tale!"

Chapter 26

The wind stirred fallen leaves on the ground beneath autumn painted trees in a little-used clearing beyond sight of the Huntsmen Headquarters compound. Thunder crashed, shaking tree branches and causing a fresh shower of leaves. Nate's Lycos appeared. Leaves blew against his legs, quickly burying his feet and ankles in red, gold, and brown. He stood silent, only his eyes moving and his ears twitching. *Good. No one knows I'm here.* He shimmered into his human form, then called his wolf to be two.

Eyes closed, Nate mentally reached through space and pulled warriors provided by each Alpha or Queen in the kingdom to him. As each group appeared, Koreth gave them instructions and sent them on their way, leaving room for new groups to come. Within the hour, the entire compound was surrounded by wolves, panthers, bears, lions, foxes, and more *were*. All awaited his signal.

Eli and his warriors were the last to arrive. Nate raised an eyebrow when he saw Renate with them. Before he could speak, Eli widened his eyes and shook his head. Nate smothered his grin. "Everyone is going in as *were*. I will go in as Lycos."

The relief on Eli's face caused Nate's lips to twitch. "Couldn't get her to stay home, huh?"

"She's a better warrior than anyone else in my pack," Eli muttered. "She insisted, and I couldn't say no."

Renate swatted Eli's arm. "Whenever you go into danger, I'm going with you."

Nate laughed, keeping it soft and low. "Take care of

yourselves. Mom and Dad will never forgive me if anything happens to either of you." His face dropped all mirth. "Eli, I don't quite trust some of these *were*. I want you and your team to search the barracks and gather any Huntsmen not in the courtyard."

"You think they might take the opportunity to get revenge and call it unavoidable?"

"They might. Let's prevent that if we can. Renate, when we get them all rounded up, you're in charge of the women." Nate glanced at Eli. "You're her backup."

Eli nodded. "Everything ready?"

"It's time. Let's go."

Eli and Renate shimmered into wolves, then led their pack warriors to the place Koreth directed. Nate watched them go while giving a silent prayer that this would work. After pulling Koreth back inside, he shifted to Lycos. *Now!*

At his mental command, the *were* animals surged out of the brush into the compound courtyard. Some Huntsmen shouted an alarm, while others screamed in terror. The humans tried to run into the buildings around them, but the *were* herded them like cattle until all stood in two tight groups divided by gender surrounded by growling, threatening animals. Lycos teleported to the center of the compound. Thunder crashed, lightning flashed, and smoke sifted through the air until it thinned enough the Huntsmen could see him.

An alarm klaxon sounded over the speakers. *Were* animals howled and humans screamed. Lycos raised a palm toward one of the speakers. Blue lightning jumped from his palm to the speaker, causing it to explode.

Jagged blue lightning buzzed and sizzled along the wires until all the speakers on the system exploded one after the other. The klaxon stopped, leaving only the sound of confused and frightened Huntsmen.

Nate's Lycos turned in a slow circle, his gaze touching each group of captured human Huntsmen. "Silence!" The power in his shout stripped the ability to speak from the Huntsmen. "I am Lycos, Royal *Were* King. This base, and others like it around the world, are ordered to shut down. You are my prisoners. No one will harm you unless you first harm one of us."

He turned to Jabril, Eli's wolf. "Retrieve anyone hiding inside the barracks. Do not kill unless you must."

Jabril bowed to Nate, then barked commands to his team. Salena, Renate's wolf, followed close behind Jabril when he ran to the first building. Unable to open the door with wolf paws, Jabril shimmered into Eli, turned the knob, and stepped inside. His wolf team followed him.

Nate sent other teams into the other buildings. Turning his attention back to the *were* with him, Nate called Zoe's and Daryll's bears to him. When the bears approached, Nate sent them a thought command to find the children and protect them. Bowing their massive heads, they turned and ran toward the class building, roaring at any Huntsman who stepped in their path.

Chapter 27

In bear form, Zoe and Daryll raced to the Huntsman class building, threading through other *were* as needed. Zoe's sensitive ears still ached from the sirens that briefly sounded. *Nate's work*, she thought. When they reached the class building, a Huntsman stepped from the entrance and raised a crossbow, taking aim at Merka, Zoe's bear. Darcel, Daryll's bear, roared, jumped ahead of her, and swatted the Huntsman with his massive paw, slamming the man into the outside wall. The human struck hard enough to dent the metal siding, then crumpled to the ground. Merka shimmered into Zoe, then she kissed Darcel's furry face.

"Thank you, Love."

At his bearish rumble, she laughed, turned, and opened the door into the building. The glass door swung open, flashing the reflection of her wearing a Huntsman uniform in the glass and she grinned. Not for the first time, she appreciated Nate insisting all *were* learned how to shift bringing their clothes with them. Running through the building naked wasn't something she would be happy doing. She let the door swing shut behind Darcel.

A whisper came from the first classroom. "Zoe?"

At the sound of her name, Zoe whipped toward an open door. A teenager peeked around the side of the door. "Lila?" Zoe took a step toward her and stopped when Lila's blue eyes widened with terror. Calmly, Zoe rested her hand on Darcel's shoulder. "It's okay. Darcel won't hurt you."

Lila stared at Zoe's fingers ruffling bear fur, then turned her gaze to Zoe. "Where have you been? Are...are you a wolf?"

Beyond Lila, behind the classroom desks, soft sobs and frantic heartbeats indicated more students were hiding. Biting her lip, Zoe took another step toward Lila. At sixteen, Lila was not yet old enough to join the Huntsmen on their missions. She was still in training, learning to hate and fear the *were* through the lies of false history taught in her classes. Even so, she was a Huntsman and trained to fight. With that in mind, Zoe took another cautious step. "I'm not a wolf. Where are the children, Lila?"

Lila took a step back, her head barely shaking in refusal to speak. Gaze on Darcel, her chin trembled.

"It's okay, Lila. We won't hurt you. We just want to release the children the Commanders ordered kidnapped. Where are they?"

Lila glanced over her shoulder at the other teens hiding behind desks, then looked at Zoe. "They said you died. You're compromised."

Zoe sighed. *There's no time to convince her.* "Stay in the classroom and lock the doors. Don't open it until I come back."

"Where are you going?"

"To the basement to find the children."

Biting her lip, Lila glanced again behind her, then frowned at Zoe. "If you go down there, they'll kill the kids to prevent them from being changed."

"They won't be changed."

"You're sure?"

At the fear in Lila's eyes, Zoe nodded. "You have my word. They won't be changed."

Lila swallowed hard, then whispered, "Take the back stairs." She slipped a key into Zoe's hand. "The front is well-guarded."

Zoe squeezed her fingers, then motioned for her to return to the classroom. Lila pulled the door shut, and the lock clicked. With a quick glance at Darcel, Zoe rushed to the back stairs. Turning the key slowly to prevent the lock from clicking as it disengaged, she took a deep breath, let it out, then gently turned the doorknob. Thankful the Huntsmen kept door hinges in good repair, Zoe slipped through the door and crept down the stairs.

She stepped off the last stair tread and quietly moved to hide behind the furnace. A light electrical charge brushed against her shoulders and she turned to see Darcel shimmer into Daryll. He moved up behind her. His hands rested on her shoulders. Casting him a quick smile, she turned back to inspect the room beyond.

He put his mouth close to her ear and murmured too softly for human hearing. "Take the lead. I'll provide backup."

She nodded. A headcount told her twenty children were sitting against the far wall, most of them scrunched down into as small a ball as they were able, their eyes closed. Three of the older kids, though scrunched like the others, had their heads up, peering fearfully at the three Huntsmen crouched behind an overturned table watching the door at the front of the room. Soft sniffles brushed against Zoe's ears, and she frowned. The Huntsmen had them terrified. The center of the floor was covered in sleeping bags.

Two of the three men held crossbows, silver quarrels cocked and ready to fire. The third held a pistol. All watched the front entrance, evidently believing the locked door behind them would give them a warning if anyone came that way. Removing her pistol from the holster, she motioned for Daryll to stay put, then quietly walked forward. The three kids saw her, their eyes opening wide. When she put a finger to her lips, they stayed quiet, watching her as she moved from one sleeping bag to another to soften her footsteps.

She stopped a few feet from the three men, her gun still in her hand. "See anything?"

The man holding the pistol shook his head. "No, they..." Glancing at her, he froze when he saw Zoe's gun aimed at him. "Zoe!"

The two others whipped around, raising their crossbows. Daryll's deep voice held a growl. "I wouldn't do that."

Zoe raised an eyebrow. "Drop your weapons. You won't be harmed in any way."

"You're compromised!" The man closest to Zoe pulled the crossbow trigger. "Die, wolf!" he shouted at the same time a high-pitched twang sounded.

Daryll was moving even before Zoe knew it. His lumberjack-sized hand shoved her to the side. The quarrel buried in his shoulder. Roaring in pain, he shifted into Darcel. His huge paw swiped the man, claws digging deep into the man's face and throat. Before the Huntsman's scream completed, the man was unconscious, bleeding on the floor. Darcel dropped on his haunches and pawed at the quarrel in his shoulder.

Behind her, children echoed the man's scream. Ignoring the kids, Zoe spun, knocking the pistol from the first man's hand, then kicking the third in the stomach. His crossbow twanged, the quarrel barreling into the wall above the children's heads. She aimed her pistol at the two still conscious. "Move again and die!" Eyes wide, they froze.

"Against the wall. Now!" When they backed away until their shoulders hit the wall, Zoe dropped to one knee. She picked up the Huntsman's pistol, snapped the safety on, then tucked it into the back of her jeans. As she stood, she kicked the two crossbows to the back of the room. Keeping her eyes on her two prisoners, Zoe backed up until she was even with Darcel.

"If you move, I will kill you." Satisfied she could react before they did if they moved, she glanced at Darcel. Blood welled from the wound. "Quit pulling at that, Darcel. You're making it worse."

Darcel roared, then grumbled. His forepaws thumped to the floor.

"Keep your eyes on them," she told Darcel, motioning toward the men with her pistol. "I'll get it out."

Darcel growled and his glowing eyes turned toward the men. Zoe dropped her pistol in the holster. Taking hold of the quarrel with both hands, she gave him a sympathetic look, then jerked as hard as she could. Darcel's roar was just slightly less intense than the screech of a jet engine. Zoe slipped on a sleeping bag. Her back slapped the floor. Bloody quarrel in her hand, she looked up at Darcel. He roared again, then shimmered into Daryll.

Zoe rolled to her feet. "Are you okay?"

Daryll coughed once, then nodded. "I will be. Silver isn't poisonous to me, but that doesn't keep it from hurting." He glanced at the crying, cowering kids. As the bleeding stopped, he sighed. Standing, he rolled his shoulder and winced when the wound pulled. He jerked his chin toward the two men hugging the wall. "Let's tie them up, then see what we can do to calm the kids."

Chapter 28

Nate swished his Lycos' wolfish tail and turned to supervise the *were* attack. While Merka and Darcel raced for the class building, teams of shifters surged into the other buildings. Shouts inside the buildings were replaced by growling as the *were* herded the people inside out the front door. A few minutes later, Eli led his team back outside. He nodded toward Nate before moving to the next barracks building. Another team moved the Huntsmen they found to the center of the compound into the appropriate gender-based group.

Dusty and Jonathan rushed into the armory. Several gunshots sounded, then they stopped. Ezrath, Jonathan's wolf, forced the Huntsmen in the armory into the center of the compound. Dusty stayed behind to guard the weapons.

General Brighton marched through the *were* to the humans, a bullhorn in his hand. Three platoons of Marines marched behind him. Brighton stopped beside Nate's Lycos. "Problems?"

"Not much. We haven't found the Triumvirate, though. According to what Lee and Peyton said, they'll probably be in the Admin building." Nate glanced at him, his wolfish eyes glowing. "Take charge out here, and I'll go find them."

Brighton nodded, turned to the Huntsmen, and raised the bullhorn to his lips. "Sit down!" His amplified command quietened the screams of the Huntsmen. They turned to find a Marine General barking orders at them.

Uniformed Marines fanned out and surrounded the two groups, rifles held ready, but muzzles pointed at the ground. Astonishment on their faces, the Huntsmen sat.

"Looks like they didn't expect the military, General."

Brighton harrumphed. "I got this. You do what you need to do."

Nate glanced at the frightened hunters, then nodded, and stalked toward the Admin building, the grounds trembling with each of his pounding footsteps.

Chapter 29

Silent, Supreme Commander Reyes watched the *were* round up his Huntsmen, then start going building to building to find more. Briefly, his eyes closed, and he swallowed. *It's over. We've lost.*

Behind him, chairs scooted away from the table, metal rollers rumbling against the tile floor. Footsteps approached, and he felt the presence of his subcommanders, one at each side. For long moments, no one spoke, then Subcommander Richter muttered, "The helicopter."

When Richter turned and ran to the door, Subcommander Vogt followed him. Reyes ignored them. There was no escape from the Lycos. The door slammed shut. Reyes still didn't move. His gaze was trapped by the magnificent wolfman approaching the Admin building. The helicopter engine whined, and the rotors chuffed through the air.

Lycos stopped his approach and looked up. He snarled, his fearful teeth showing. As the helicopter rose from the roof, Lycos raised a clawed hand and threw blue lightning at it. From the window, Reyes couldn't see the helicopter, but the explosion that destroyed it shook the building. Glass shattered. Shards embedded into his face, chest, and shoulders. Filtered light from beneath the canopy followed the blast. Overhead, the weight of the copter crashed into the roof. The smell of hot metal, burning flesh, and melting plastic filled the air.

Reyes squinted against the light and released the

breath he was holding. Watching Lycos throw blue light at the rooftop again, he absently brushed glass from his bloodless wounds and clothes. The roar of flames over his head suddenly ceased. *Lycos put the fire out.* Reyes walked back to the command table. Picking up the sunglasses he earlier dropped on the table, he settled them over his eyes. *No escape.* Calmly, he sat at the table, facing the door.

*****

Nate stopped outside the Commanders Office and shimmered into his human form. Not knowing how many were in the helicopter he destroyed, he didn't know if anyone would be inside. *One vampire waits inside.* He nodded at Koreth's thought and opened the door. Stepping inside, he stopped, facing the vampire sitting at the table. Nate raised an eyebrow but stayed silent.

The vampire swallowed, blinked, then his shoulders steadied. He stared at Nate. Slowly, the vampire stood. "You are Lycos."

Nate gave him a shallow nod. "I am."

Eyes hidden by the shades he wore, the vampire sighed. "You wear the crown."

"You can see it?" Nate thought the vampire wouldn't answer, but after a moment, he gave him a single nod.

"What happens now?"

Nate studied the vampire. Taller than most humans, the slender man looked too emaciated to be a threat. *He's more dangerous than he looks.* Nate agreed with Koreth's assessment. "Now, we walk out of here. You are under arrest for crimes against *were* and humanity."

"Is it a crime for the wolf to kill a deer? It is his nature. I have done nothing outside my nature."

"You have killed many. The Progenitors forbid consuming human blood, yet you enslave humans to feed you." Nate waved his fingers in the air in a come-hither motion. "Come with me."

"And if I refuse."

Nate's patience evaporated. "You die. Here. Now."

Chapter 30

The clowder queen's representatives in the battle, Marcel and Eachann, Ben's and Will's panthers, stalked into the gymnasium. Marcel sniffed. Dozens of humans hid beneath the bleachers. Beside him, Eachann shimmered into a human.

"We won't hurt you," Will called. "Come out and sit on the bleachers."

A furtive movement pulled Marcel's gaze to the far end of the bleachers on his left. Gun! He roared and shoved Will toward the floor. The shot reverberated through the building, mixed with human screams. The bullet aimed at Will's heart struck his forehead. Blood splattered, then splattered again when Will hit the floor.

Marcel didn't stop to see if Will lived. The panther snarled and hissed, then pounced at the man turning the gun on him. Again, the gun bucked in the man's hand. Before Marcel smelled the gunpowder, hot pain blasted through his left upper foreleg as he crashed to the floor, the man beneath him.

The man screamed. Marcel's huge jaws closed over his neck and ripped out his throat. With a gurgling gasp, the man shuddered, then lay still. Snarling, Marcel rose to his feet and turned to face the humans hiding behind the bleachers. The stink of their fear caused his eyes to water. Snatching the gun in his jaws, he threw it to the far end of the building, then turned to look again at the humans. Shuddering with pain, he shimmered into a human.

Ben glanced at the wound in his bicep. The bullet went

completely through the muscle, but the silver would have to be cleaned out for it to heal properly. Even if it wasn't as poisonous to him as it was to wolves, silver did affect him. Cursing under his breath, he ripped a section from his t-shirt and clumsily tied it around the wound. He frowned at the humans. *Teens. They're just teens!* "Get on the bleachers and sit still." When they didn't move, he let the panther show in his eyes. "Now!"

Tripping over each other, the teens rushed to the bleachers. Sitting, they clung to each other. All save one young man who glared at Ben, belligerence in the set of his lips and the angle of his jaw. Ben growled at him. "Don't move." Fear touched the boy's eyes.

Ben rushed to Will and gently turned the unconscious man over. Ripping another strip from his shirt, Ben used gentle fingers to dab away the blood. Already the bleeding slowed. If the wound wasn't serious, Will would be awake by now. Ben touched the radio on his belt. "We need medics in the gym. Panther down."

A furtive movement caught his attention. The belligerent boy shifted slowly toward the end of the bleachers. Ben didn't shout, but the dead flat voice coming from his mouth frightened him almost as much as it frightened the teens. "This man is my daughter's intended mate. The only reason you are alive is you didn't pull the trigger. If I have to leave his side to deal with you, you are dead. Get. Back. To. The. Others."

Something in the flat declaration must have gotten through. The boy froze, then slowly stood, walked back to the group, and sat down. Ben watched until he sat, then turned his attention back to his future son-in-law. Time seemed to slow to a crawl, but finally, he heard the medivac helicopter land outside the building. The gym door crashed against the wall and two medics rushed toward him. He moved back to give them room to work.

Ben ignored the whispers between the kids sitting on the bleachers, more concerned with Will. After several minutes of working with him, a medic took a collapsible stretcher from his pack and unfolded it. The two soldiers carefully lifted Will onto the stretcher. Set their pack on Will's legs, then carried him out. Ben swallowed. *If he dies, Flora...* He shook off the thought. Fixing his gaze on the teens, he motioned toward the door. "Let's go."

"Where?" The belligerent kid seemed determined to annoy him. "What are you? You're no wolf."

"I'm a panther, and I'm getting tired of your mouth. All of you, get out the door and join your friends."

Sniffles punctuated the whispers. One of the girls stood. "Are you making us wolves, or panthers, or...or whatever?"

"No. If you don't attack us, you won't be harmed. If you attack..." Ben waved toward the dead man behind him without taking his gaze from her. "If you attack, you'll be stopped. If you hurt someone, you die. What's your name?"

"Stacy." She swallowed and slapped the back of the belligerent boy's head. "Let's go, Vince."

"They're going to kill us. Or worse."

"Maybe. Maybe not." She glanced at the door when it opened again.

Zoe entered and walked to Ben. "The classrooms are cleared. How's Will?"

"Don't know, yet, but I think it's pretty bad." He motioned again to the kids. "I said, let's go."

Zoe put her hand on his arm. "May I?"

Annoyed, Ben glanced down at her, then nodded. "I'd rather not hurt anyone else."

"Zoe?" Stacy's soft voice trembled.

Zoe looked at the Huntsman girl. "Hello, Stacy." She held up a hand to stop the questions suddenly bursting from the group of teens. "No, I'm not a wolf." She winked at Ben, then gazed at Stacy. "And I'm not a panther. I've been with these guys since I left here." Without changing her focus, she waved a hand at Ben. "I've learned some things you don't know. These guys won't hurt you. It's their job to protect you."

Vince shook his head. "He killed Jack."

"Jack shot his friend and daughter's mate. If he intended to hurt you, you'd all be dead by now. There's nothing you could do to stop him."

"I have my knife." Vance's voice held a threat.

Ben snorted and Zoe shook her head. "Silver isn't poisonous to panthers, Vance. You might wound him temporarily, but you'd still die."

"Hush, Vance." Stacy jumped off the bleachers to face Zoe. "I don't understand. It's his job to protect us from what?"

"Vampires." When the kids exchanged incredulous looks, Zoe sighed.

Ben could feel her reluctance to be the one to tell them. He took a step forward and briefly glanced at each of them. "Look at your friends. Really look at them. Study their necks. You will see slight scars. You all have them.

The Triumvirate Commanders are vampires using you to destroy the only creatures on Earth that can keep them from enslaving all humans as food animals. You've all fed them."

Disbelief in their expressions, they turned to glance at their neighbor's necks. Their faces showed startled surprise, then fear, then anger. When Zoe spoke, they turned their agitated attention to her. "The *were* are tasked with protecting humans from vampires that would enslave them. We are here to free you from them. For now, please follow orders. Most of you know me. I promise you won't be harmed unless you hurt one of the *were*. Please," she turned sideways and gestured toward the door, "go outside and sit with the other Huntsmen."

Chapter 31

Supreme Commander Reyes marched out of the Admin building to the center of the compound grounds, the *Were* King behind him. A man wearing a Marine General's uniform finished giving orders over his radio and turned to face them. Reyes step faltered and he jerked to a stop. "What...?"

The general crossed his arms over his chest and stared at Reyes. He glanced at the *Were* King. "The others?"

"Died in the helicopter. This one's all yours, General."

Reyes glanced back at the man behind him. "He's with you?"

"We work together."

"Bravo and Charley have control of the ranch, Nate," the General said.

The man the general called Nate nodded, then glanced at the skies. "It's going to rain. Is that canopy going to provide shelter?"

"It should, but we can move inside just in case."

"Sounds good. The only building large enough to house everyone at once is the gym. Send a squad in to search it for hidden arms. When it's clear, move everyone in there."

The General turned. "Alpha squad."

A soldier stepped to the front and saluted. "Sir."

"Search the gym."

With another salute, the soldier led ten men to the gym. In less than ten minutes, they returned. "All clear, Sir!"

"Move'em in, Lieutenant."

*****

Without waiting for orders, Zoe accompanied the Huntsmen. None of the humans saw her as Merka, so she was hoping her presence would help. Daryll's scent followed her into the gym. She noticed Will's blood was cleaned up, no doubt by the soldiers, and Jack's body was gone. Single file, the Huntsmen climbed up the bleachers, filling them completely, then the remaining humans sat on the gym floor in front of the bleachers.

After they were all seated, the door opened and Nate walked in, the General behind him. Two soldiers followed, each holding one of the Supreme Commander's arms. The General and his men stopped on the three-point line, while Nate continued to center court. Zoe blinked at the incongruity of a basketball court containing armed soldiers, werewolves, and vampires. She stood in front of the Huntsmen, Daryll at her side. At Nate's gesture, she and Daryll walked to stand behind the soldiers.

"My name is Nate Rollins. And, yes, I'm a wolf."

His announcement sent murmurs and stirs of fear through the crowd. Zoe's gaze moved across the crowd, trying to show them there was nothing to fear. Some of the Huntsmen's eyes narrowed as they searched for a way to escape.

"But I am more than a wolf. I am Lycos." Nate shimmered into his Lycos form. Cries erupted from the crowd. "Silence."

Nate's soft command brought instant quiet. The Huntsmen cowered when even their voices obeyed him.

"I am the *Were* King, King of all *Were* on Earth. My charter is to protect humans from V-Triumph, rogue vampires that feed on humans." He shimmered into his human form. At his motion, the General led his men to stand next to Nate. "Your Supreme Commander is V-Triumph. A vampire who feeds on humans."

Nate glanced at Reyes. "Show your true self."

Reyes glared at him. "There is nothing to show."

Nate jerked his head at Brighton. Brighton changed. His face paled and fangs distended below his bottom lip. His eyes glowed a sickly whitish yellow. He took a step and clasped Reyes' neck in his massive clawed hand. With a jerk, he threw the other vampire to the floor. Snarling, he took a step toward Reyes. "Show yourself or die as a human would in your hands."

Fury filled Reyes' face. His eyes glimmered into a whitish yellow glow and his face paled. His fangs distended just as the General's had. Roaring a challenge, he surged to his feet, clawed hands reaching for Brighton. Brighton spun aside, then stood straight. Nate's right hand morphed into Lycos' clawed hand and grasped the back of Reyes' neck. Lifting the vampire off the floor, Nate shook him, until he stopped moving. He tossed the vampire back to the waiting hands of his guards, then his hand reformed into a human hand.

Nate turned to face the humans. "Your Supreme Commander Reyes is V-Triumph, a vampire assigned to control the Huntsmen in this location. You were told the Huntsmen were formed to destroy *were* to safeguard humans. What you have not been told is after the *were* are gone, you will be their slaves. Food bred solely to feed the vampires."

Mutters washed through the room. One of the older Huntsmen stood. "Why would we believe a wolf?"

"We will free your minds from the compulsion laid upon you. You will remember all that has happened to you since you came to this place." His powerful gaze swept over them. Zoe swallowed. She knew how that felt.

"Before that, however, your Supreme Commander's trial begins."

"Trial?" Reyes' fangs glistened in the indoor lighting. "Who dares? You? You haven't the authority!"

"But I know someone who does." Nate bowed his head, eyes closed for a moment. When he raised his head, Zoe was surprised to see clouds forming and billowing in the gym. The entire basketball court was covered. A brilliant flash of violet light speared her eyes, then violet clouds boiled behind Nate. As they began to dissipate, he turned to face them and dropped to one knee. A woman stepped out of the clouds. Long dark hair draped over her glowing violet gown. Her dark eyes scanned the room. She raised an eyebrow when she saw Reyes, then turned to face Nate.

Beside Nate, the general also dropped to one knee, his head bowed. The *were*, including the two soldiers holding the prisoner, kneeled and bowed their heads, forcing Reyes to his knees, too. Daryll's hand found Zoe's and pulled her down. She glanced at him, but his reverently bowed head suggested she should follow suit. Bowing, she waited for...she didn't know what she waited for. Behind her, she heard the humans catch their breaths. Zoe risked a peek to see them all staring at the woman, some of them with open mouths.

"You have summoned me, Son of my Son's Son?" The musical quality of her voice held Zoe enthralled.

Coming to his feet, Nate nodded toward Reyes. "I have captured one of those who defy the Progenitors, First Mother."

The woman faced Reyes. Light glowed in her eyes, and the vampire raised his chin, his arrogance on display. "What have you to say for yourself, Vampire?"

"I defy the Progenitor's right to forbid my nature." Reyes jerked his arms from the soldiers and stood, his eyes blazing sickly yellow.

"Your nature is to consume blood, true, but it is not to consume human blood. The blood of humans was unknown to your people before you came to this Earth. You refuse to redeem yourself?"

Reyes took a threatening step toward her. "I refuse. You killed my grandfather for feeding. For that, you will die!" He leaped toward her. As his feet left the ground, she flashed her palm at him. Dark purple light splashed into him and stopped him mid-air. He struggled above the clouds covering the floor. "For your refusal, you are condemned! By Lycos' hand, you were captured. By Lycos' hand, you will die!"

Nate shimmered into Lycos. He raised his hands and caught hold of the vampire's ears. "So commands the First Mother." The same blue lightning he threw at the speakers earlier surged from his palms.

The vampire's agonized scream brought bile up Zoe's throat, but the Supreme Commander had killed Stacy Ann while she watched. He sent her to kill Paige, her best friend, and Paige's entire family, knowing Zoe would die, too. Only Nate prevented that. Reyes was responsible for destroying unknown numbers of wolf and human families. She steeled herself and watched, knowing he deserved his judgment.

For long minutes, the light bore into Reyes, getting brighter and brighter, then with a final shriek, he seemed to evaporate in mid-air. The light retreated. Zoe blinked. Tears, not for the man but from the sting of the bright light hitting her eyes, slipped down her cheeks. Surprised, she dashed the back of her hand across her face to wipe them away.

"It is done." The low, guttural quality of Nate's Lycos voice took her gaze to him. He dropped again to one knee and bowed to the First Mother. Zoe again peeked at her.

The First Mother glanced at the crowd and sighed. "All these are victims of the lesser vampires."

She raised her hand, curling her fingers into a crescent moon shape. She drew her hand across her body, chest high from left to right, then turned her wrist and pointed her flattened palm at the ceiling. Light, a pure ethereal violet color, flowed from her palm to the rafters, splashed against the ceiling, then gently fell in shimmering flakes over the entire crowd. Human voices gasped and murmured.

Zoe glanced at the Huntsmen. They knew. Somehow, the First Mother removed the vampire's compulsions. She could see in their faces that they remembered all they had seen, all they had suffered at the hands of their commanders. Soft sobs sounded through the crowd, and the Huntsmen turned to their friends and family for comfort. Zoe swallowed, knowing exactly how they felt.

"Arise."

Zoe looked again at the First Mother and watched as she touched the shoulders of both Nate and General Brighton. Her smile turned to the general. "You have done well in this struggle, Young One. Your efforts will be rewarded."

Brighton bowed his head. "I have no need of reward, Milady. I serve to fulfill the Ancient's bidding."

She smiled and turned to Nate. "Son of my Son's Son, this battle is won, but the war continues. There are still rebellious vampires in this world, threatening both humankind and werekind. Your charge remains. Protect human and *were* from the vampires who wish them harm."

"As you command, First Mother." He, too, bowed his head.

She glanced again at the general. "Young One, your duty is to serve the Royal *Were* King as he needs for the protection of human and *were*. Do you accept this?"

"As you command, First Mother," said the general and bowed, following Nate's lead.

"So be it. I leave this world of my beginning to your charge, Son of my Son's Son. Protect it well. Should you have need, summon me." Purple mist swirled through the air, enveloping her. When the mist fell away, First Mother was gone.

Chapter 32

As night fell, Nate released the humans to their homes and barracks. All had given their pledge to the Royal *Were* King to help in the fight against V-Triumph. Some preferred to spend some time with family, while others were determined to help destroy V-Triumph. They were so lost and confused, Peyton volunteered to return to Headquarters to help the Huntsmen restructure their lives. Lee offered to help him.

Nate, Lee, Peyton, General Brighton, and the members of his council on-site gathered in the Commander's Office and sat at the command table. General Brighton dropped a stack of applications on the table. "So far, we have over two hundred applications to join the Special Forces unit."

Nate tapped the table with his thumb. "How many will you accept?"

"After verifying they don't have residual loyalty to the Huntsmen, all of them." Brighton sighed. "We have a long war ahead of us. Huntsmen have enclaves in Germany, China, India, South Africa, Brazil, and Canada, as well as other places. It will take time to route the V-Triumph, since we must protect the human Huntsmen, where possible."

"Did the Pentagon ever give you a base for operations?"

At Nate's question, Brighton raised an eyebrow. "We barely get enough funds to have a unit at all."

"That's what I thought." Nate steepled his hands and

leaned back in his chair. "General, there is a perfectly good base right here. Why don't you take over here and start training the Special Forces we are going to need over the next few years."

General Brighton blinked. "How do we fund it?"

Nate shrugged. "I'm sure the Huntsmen have some way to fund their operations here. Take it over. If you still need funds, let me know. I'll have each *were* group in the kingdom to 'donate' say, 1% of their profits. That should be enough to cover a lot of needs." He grinned. "You would get a good bit of change just from the ranch earnings. Lee and Peyton will be here to help you."

"Paige will come, too, though I think Phillip will prefer to stay at the ranch." Peyton smiled. "He's more suited to ranch life than military life." On Peyton's left, a silly grin covered Lee's face.

When Lee flushed, Nate briefly grinned. Turning to Ben, he dropped the grin. "How's Will?"

"The general's doctor says he will live. There may be some brain damage. He's not healing as well as expected due to the silver in the bullet. While it's not poisonous to him, it left traces of silver that scarred. We won't know until he finishes healing." Ben twitched and cleared his throat. "I'd like to take Will home to Flora, but the doctors don't want him to move for at least a week."

With a frown, Nate studied the misery in his former police captain's face. "Call Flora and tell her to be ready in an hour. I'll bring her here to be with him. Later tonight I'll come by and see if there's anything I can do to help him."

"Thank you, Nate. I appreciate it."

Nate gave an absent nod. He glanced at Jonathan. "Inform the Ambassadors that we will have a full meeting at the ranch on Tuesday at 2 pm. I think it's time we took a more formal approach to this problem." He rolled his chair back, then walked to the glassless window. Watching the humans walking to their homes or barracks, he frowned. "The *were*, too, need to be better trained. Perhaps it is time for a formal school for shifters."

Chapter 33

While the changes in Nate's life often annoyed him, he accepted his kingship and responsibilities as gracefully as he could. Over the next two weeks, Nate met with the Representatives of the World Enclave, working out the format of the Royal *Were* Government. There were times, though, especially during the pompous speeches given by assorted Representatives that Nate wished it would all just go away. Sometimes, the only thing that kept him going was Janelle's support.

Since Will was finally on his feet, but still not feeling one-hundred percent, Ben took over Will's duties in addition to his own. Even *were* had trouble recuperating from severe brain injuries. Nate was just glad the man was alive. He settled into his office chair and released a deep sigh. An envelope was on his desk. Eyebrow raised, he opened it. Flora sent him an invitation to her and Will's wedding. In an enclosed note, Flora wrote, "I'm not waiting anymore. I can't risk letting this get away from us." Nate grinned his approval. There was nothing like a wedding to bring joy to the *were*. Progenitor knew they were due some joy and happiness.

Staring at the invitation, he thought of his own wedding to Janelle. Even now, he considered it the best day of his life, followed closely by the day Ophelia was born. Janelle made him promise to make Ophelia's life as normal as he could. She was right. At Janelle's insistence, nothing in the household changed. She might be Queen, but she was first the Pack Mother, with all the responsibilities of that title, including overseeing the cooking and cleaning and raising their daughter. Nate had no desire to tell her what to do or what her life must be. If she wanted to change it, so be it. If not, that was okay, too.

He rolled his head, stretching his neck. A glance at the clock told him it was almost supper time. *That's good. I'm starved!* He sniffed and a grin covered his face. *Lasagna!*

Soft footsteps raced up the stairs. Minutes later, Janelle's distress hit his mind. He jumped up, shoving his chair into the windowsill behind him. Jerking the door open, he found Janelle standing at the bedroom door, looking in, her hands clasped over her mouth. Frowning, he moved behind her and gently grasped her shoulders. Not knowing if Ophelia was sleeping, he kept his voice soft. "What's going on? What's wrong?"

*****

When Lisa walked into the kitchen, Janelle took the second pan of lasagna from the oven and looked at the young teen. With a frown, she shut the oven door and set the pan on the counter next to the first pan. "Where's Ophelia?"

Pink bloomed in Lisa's face, and guilt glimmered in her eyes. "I just came to get a drink."

Janelle fixed the Pack Mother glare on the girl. "Uh huh. Where's Ophelia?"

Lisa swallowed. "She's in the nursery. Mason's with her."

"Mason Neville? Little guy?"

"Y...yes, Ma'am."

"And you thought it was a good idea to leave the Princess alone with a seven-year-old?"

Licking her lips, Lisa swallowed again. "Mason's ten. He won't hurt her, Janelle."

Janelle gave an exasperated huff and rushed up the stairs, her sneaker-clad feet making little noise. Opening the nursery door, she stopped. Ophelia sat on the floor, giggling at Mason and clapping her hands. Mason bowed to her, then sat cross-legged in front of her. He gave Ophelia the stuffed rabbit she reached for, then smiled at her. The adoration on the boy's face stunned Janelle. Ophelia bounced with excitement, dropped the rabbit, and crawled toward Mason. Giggling with her, Mason scooted closer and pulled Ophelia into his lap. Ophelia settled against him. Mason pressed his face against the top of her head, rocked from side-to-side, and sang a soft lullaby.

Hands covering her mouth, Janelle leaned against the door frame and watched as Ophelia's eyes drifted closed. Within moments, she was asleep. *How can Mason get her to go to sleep so easily?* Janelle was startled at Nadrai's response. *He is her chosen one.* With a jerk, Janelle stood straight. *They're too young to mate!* Nadrai's laughter rippled through Janelle's mind. *But not too young to find their future mates.*

Until Nate left the office and stepped up behind her, Janelle did not realize she was broadcasting her distress. His broad hands clasped her shoulders. "What's going on? What's wrong?"

At his soft voice, Janelle glanced over her shoulder at him and sighed. "Looks like Ophelia's Prince found her."

"What?" Nate's chest pressed against her back as he leaned forward to look past her into the nursery.

They will bond when they are grown. Janelle heard Koreth's thought affirm Nadrai's assessment.

The startled look Nate sent Janelle mirrored her feelings. He kept his words soft. "But they're just children!"

They will grow. He must be trained to be our successor.

At Koreth's thought, Nate raised an eyebrow. *The boy is a panther!*

Janelle frowned at him. *There is no place in this pack for racism. Of any kind.*

"You're right. I'm sorry. More than anything, I was surprised," he murmured, the heat of shame touching his cheeks. Nate's embarrassment brushed against Janelle's mind.

Koreth thought, *Fate has chosen to mate Ophelia with him.*

Nate's hand clenched Janelle's sweater. Janelle placed her palm on Nate's hand. She gave him a gentle shove to move him out of the nursery doorway, then quietly closed the door and turned to face him. "It's not common, Nate, but mating across bloodlines isn't forbidden. It might be what we need to ensure the success of the next *Were* King's reign."

His gaze searched her face. "You're okay with this?" The red in his face deepened. "Not with him being a panther. With them choosing so young?"

Janelle studied his expression. "If they are true mates, we can't prevent it." Janelle caught his hand in both hers. "How would you feel if someone decided we couldn't be together?"

Understanding dawned in his eyes.

"As *were*, we can't fight it. What we can do is provide him the training and support he will need when it is time for him to become the *Were* King. Or at the very least, Consort to the *Were* Queen."

Nate let out a long breath. "Would've been nice if someone had done that for me."

"They did. Your parents and Dusty made sure you had the physical training from your early childhood to have the ability to fight. They gave you a solid foundation, an understanding of right and wrong, good and evil. Without all that, you would not be the king you are."

Janelle watched him look at their joined hands. For a moment, tension tightened his shoulders, then he relaxed and nodded. "You're right. They did what they could to get me ready. Now it's our turn to get them ready." He took a deep breath and looked at the closed nursery door, then he smiled and raised her fingers to his lips. "Both of them."

derdi*Wolf's Queen* is the next book in the series.

Thank You!

Thank you for reading, *Wolf's Reign*, the sixth book in the Texas Ranch Wolf Pack series.

Please Leave a Review

Reviews are the lifeblood of books in today's market. If you read this book, please take the time to leave an honest review.

Reviews are not book reports. They are just a few words to let other readers know how you liked or didn't like the book.

Authors, especially indie authors, depend on reviews to help readers find their books. Good or bad reviews help an author on the journey as an author.

You can also find Lynn Nodima's books and stories at: www.lynnnodima.com.

Lynn's Books

The Texas Ranch Wolf Pack Series
Wolf's Man
Wolf's Claim
Wolf's Mission
Wolf's Huntsman
Wolf's Trust
Wolf's Reign
Wolf's Queen
Wolf's Enemy
Wolf's Rage
Wolf's Quest
Wolf's Guard
Wolf's Duty

Texas Ranch Wolf Pack World
Wolf's Sorrow
Wolf's Mate
Wolf's Heart
Wolf's Dragon
Wolf's Princess
Wolf's Son
Dragon's Treasure
Panther's Choice
Panther's Task
Wolf's Encounter
    (free with opt-in—visit www.lynnnodima.com for link)

Texas Ranch Wolf Pack Box Sets
Wolf's Destiny: Books 1-6
Wolf's Victory: Books 7-12

The Tala Ridge Shifters Series
Tala Ridge Alpha
Tala Ridge Storm
Tala Ridge Hunt
Tala Ridge Witch

Short Story Collections
Dreams in the Night

Short Stories
Alas, Atlantis!
All I Done
Design Defect
Heart Failure
A Relative Truth
Trinity's Sorrow
The Viper Pit

The Billionaire Brothers
Holiday Rescue
Not for Sale
Pete's Cafe (TBD)
Cuppa Brew
    (free with opt-in—visit
    https://www.lynnscleanromances.com/ for link)

Email Lynn at lynn@lynnnodima.com!

Milton Keynes UK
Ingram Content Group UK Ltd.
UKHW010747110624
444053UK00001B/20